Lizzie Flying Solo

Lizzie Flying Solo

NANCI TURNER STEVESON

HARPER
An Imprint of HarperCollins*Publishers*

Lizzie Flying Solo

 For information address HarperCollins Children's Books, a division of HarperCollins Publishers, 195 Broadway, New York, NY 10007.
www.harpercollinschildrens.com

Library of Congress Control Number: 2018954198
ISBN 978-0-06-267318-3 (trade bdg.)

Typography by Erin Fitzsimmons
19 20 21 22 23 PC/LSCH 10 9 8 7 6 5 4 3 2 1

First Edition

To those who seek shelter
And those who offer it.
And for my beloved Sarah.
This book is for you.

SUMMER

ONE

On the second to last day of June, Mom came into my room with a frown on her face and a navy-blue suitcase in her hand.

"Lizzie," she said, "we have to give our house back to the bank."

I looked up from my book. "Why does the bank want our house?"

She shifted her focus to the window.

"Is it because of Dad?"

She clenched her jaw a tiny bit, the way she always did

when that subject came up. “Yes, because of Dad. I can’t pay for it anymore.”

“Won’t they let us stay until after his trial, just to see what happens?”

“I tried. I’m really sorry. It’s just until we’re back on our feet.”

She placed the suitcase on the floor.

“Pack up the things you care about the most. Everything else will go into storage.”

“Wait, storage? Where are we going to live?”

Mom walked to the window and tied the yellow plaid curtains to the side, then stared at the red maple tree in the backyard. My grandparents’ ashes were buried under the roots of that tree. Her own parents. Mom would never leave them behind forever. She crossed her arms and turned back to me.

“We’re moving to a new town for a while. No one there will know anything about what happened. We’ll be living in a place with other people, so you can make friends again, real friends who won’t judge you the way MaryBeth and Amy did. Everyone needs a fresh start from time to time. This is our turn.”

“Mom, no. I don’t want to go. People here will forget. You said MaryBeth and Amy were reacting to rumors and that when Dad gets back everything will return to normal.”

That made her wince. “It’s not that simple, Lizzie.

Sometimes we have to answer to things we have no control over. I'm really sorry."

She hurried out the door and left the suitcase sitting square in the middle of the floor, mocking me.

For the next few hours I moved around the house, touching all the things I loved and not understanding how I could possibly pick which of them meant the most. One at a time, I flipped through the pages of my books and ran my finger across the pencil marks where I'd written my name inside. Somewhere between *Charlotte's Web* and *Black Beauty*, I'd learned to sign my name in script. The plastic horses lined up across the top of my bookcase each had names and invented life stories. From their basket in the corner, my four favorite stuffed animals watched me wander around the room. Their eyes asked the question I couldn't answer. Who did I love the best?

It was hard enough to decide what to put inside the suitcase, but how would I pack the things I couldn't touch? Like the way sunlight streamed through my windows and made tic-tac-toe patterns on the hardwood floors, or the smell of burning bacon from Saturday mornings when it was Dad's turn to cook? No navy-blue suitcase could hold those things.

Downstairs, I tested the doorknob to Dad's study to see if it was locked, wondering if there was anything inside that was important. Until a couple of years ago, Dad had always had an open-door policy: I came and went without knocking.

Back then he'd been a normal dad. We'd been a normal family, doing all the same kinds of things my friends' families did: summer cookouts, family movie night, sledding on Powder Hill. Then he got weird and started locking himself inside the study, and he'd get mad at me for trying to come in uninvited. Everything changed again when he was arrested for something that had to do with white collars, and I don't mean changed for the better. I let go of the knob. Whatever was inside that room, I didn't want it anyway.

We kept our winter clothes and ice skates packed up in the mudroom closet. I opened a bin to be sure I wasn't missing anything important. A black riding helmet toppled from the shelf above and bounced onto the floor. It was the helmet Dad had given me for Christmas, only a few days before he was arrested. In the same box was a letter from the owner of a riding stable not far away telling me I was going to start my long-dreamed-of lessons the following Thursday. I never even got to the first one, because that was the day they came and took Dad away.

I didn't see them arrest him. I barely got a glimpse of the three men standing in the foyer asking for him, because as soon as they came in, Mom grabbed me from the kitchen and practically pushed me up the stairs with firm instructions to stay in my room. But our neighbor, Mrs. Alfieri, saw the whole thing. She told me—and everyone else in town—that when they slapped those handcuffs on Dad's wrists, it was the loudest click she'd ever heard. I kicked the helmet against the wall, slammed the mudroom door shut, and ran back upstairs.

Hidden in the back of my closet was a shoe box where I kept a small pocket version of *Webster's Dictionary & Thesaurus*, a couple of sharpened pencils, and a hot-pink suede diary. That diary was nearly half filled with words I hoped to turn into real poems someday. I crawled inside the closet and sat in the corner hidden behind clothes hanging from a rod and left the door cracked just enough for a wedge of light to spread across my lap. Holding the pencil firmly against a fresh page of the diary, I waited for words to appear—words that might carry away some of the angst choking me.

After I'd scribbled and scrawled and let silent tears fall, I wrapped the diary inside a blue-and-white Middlebury College sweatshirt and dropped it into the suitcase along with my box of pencils and a sketch pad. I chose eight books, two of my plastic horses, a photo of my grandparents, all four stuffed animals, and the braided leather friendship bracelet MaryBeth had given me before she found out Dad got her father in trouble, too. I had to rearrange everything twice to squeeze in the brand-new bird feeder Mom and I had bought on the first day of spring. That was before she decided things like bird feeders were "unessential" and could no longer be purchased. The suitcase was so full, I had to sit on it to get it zippered shut.

The next morning the doorbell rang at eight o'clock. I heard Mom open the door and I went to the top of the stairs to listen. It was a bunch of people from a moving company who were packing up and taking our stuff to storage. I ran to my room to be sure I hadn't forgotten anything, something I might have overlooked the afternoon before. My suitcase was downstairs by the front door, so it would need to be something small that I could carry. Mom had already packed most of my clothes, and a quick search inside the closet showed there wasn't anything left that I'd miss over the next few months. I scanned my entire bedroom, wishing I could take the curtains with me, or the lamp, or more of my plastic horses.

Or everything.

Nothing in particular jumped out, so I snatched a miniature clay cactus plant I'd made in elementary school and pushed it down inside my jeans pocket. Then I stood in the middle of the room and watched as the sun outside made the tic-tac-toe pattern spread shadows until each pane was half as wide as one of my feet. Placing my left foot on a line, I carefully positioned my right foot in front of it, and stood awkwardly with my arms out to each side, as if I was on the balance beam in the school gym. With my eyes closed, I inhaled deeply and made a wish that we'd be home sooner rather than later.

An hour later, the movers were still working when Mom and I waited by the front door for a man from the bank who was coming to get the keys to the house and drive us to the new town. The old Toyota Mom had been rattling around in since she'd sold our regular cars had disappeared a few days before, too. She watched out the window, her eyes glazed over, staring at her prized flower garden along the front walkway. Her favorite peach-colored roses were in full bloom, and a few hung heavy with dew.

I touched her elbow gently. "Mom?"

The corner of her mouth twitched in response.

"Can I ask you something?"

"Hmmm?"

"Do you really think we'll be coming back?"

She sighed the tiniest bit but didn't shift her eyes from the flowers outside. "The law says every person is innocent until proven guilty."

Her voice sounded robotic, like she'd said those words out loud to herself a million times over.

"That's not what I asked. Do you really think we'll come back here after the trial?"

She felt around for my hand and took it in hers, then pressed both of them tight against her chest.

"I hope so, Lizzie," she said. "I really do."

TWO

When Mom said we were going to be living in a place with other people, I thought she meant we'd be moving into an apartment building, like the one where our gardener, Mr. French, lived. Every summer Mr. French had come to take care of Mom's flower beds—every summer until this one. A few years back his car wouldn't start at the end of the day, so Mom and I had driven him home.

Mr. French's town was different from ours. It had narrow, crowded streets and buildings so tall they almost blocked the sky. But when we pulled up to a redbrick apartment complex, he'd smiled and pointed to a tiny patio sticking out the side of the second story. Masses of hot-pink and purple flowers wound their way up wrought iron railings. A lady wearing an apron was clipping herbs from a tub next to a large pot of bright yellow sunflowers. She smiled and waved at us, her hand full of rosemary and mint.

"My garden, my wife," Mr. French had said, beaming.

That was the kind of place I expected for our temporary home. That, I thought, I could do until after Dad's trial. So when the man from the bank dropped us off at Good Hope: A Home for Families in Transition, I froze. It wasn't an apartment complex where each family had their own place to live. It was a single, rambling house sitting alone at the end of an otherwise lifeless street, plunked in the middle of scrub bushes and wild grasses, with two old oak trees groaning in the front yard. Cracked concrete steps led to a front door with long strips of paint peeling over the top. Three pairs of eyes watched us through a bay window as we approached. I stopped short and set my suitcase on a patch of dirt.

"Mom, no."

She didn't even look at me. "Lizzie, yes."

She lugged two suitcases up the steps, came back for a box of clothing and another labeled "Important Papers," then motioned for me to follow.

"No, I can't. *We* can't."

Her eyes pleaded with me not to argue. "We'll be safe here. Be grateful."

The reality of this new change in our lives stunned me to

silence. Mom knocked on the door, and a few seconds later it opened a crack. A lady with short dark hair and glasses peered out, then stood aside and waved us in.

"You can leave your things here for now," she said brusquely, indicating the small entryway. "We'll go over the rules, then I'll take you to your room."

Mom and I pushed all our belongings across the threshold and followed the lady down some steps to a large family-type room. Old, overstuffed couches that didn't match lined the walls, and a big TV sat on a three-sided table in one corner. There was a short bookcase stocked with *Reader's Digest* magazines, a table with a tower of board games, and the bay window looking out to the front yard. Mom sank down in one of the couches, and I sat next to her on a flaming-orange cushion covering the window seat. No sign of the people belonging to the six eyes that had watched us a few moments before.

The lady pulled up a metal folding chair and perched on the edge, sitting with her back tall and rigid. She held a clipboard close to her chest.

"I am Miss May," she said. "I am in charge of Good Hope. It is my responsibility to see to it all our residents are safe and working toward the goal of independence."

Mom nodded politely.

"You must obey the rules to be allowed to stay at Good Hope," Miss May went on.

She looked at me like she was waiting for a confession of some rule I must have already broken in the few minutes since we'd arrived. When nothing came, she handed each of us a sheet of paper with *Rules for Considerate Living* written across the top and proceeded to read each out loud.

- *No drugs, alcohol, or smoking of any kind*
- *No visitors without prior approval*
- *No lollygagging on the front steps*
- *No children outside after dark*
- *No children touching the stove, oven, or refrigerator*
- *No alterations in your room (paint, picture hangers/nails/coat hooks bolted into walls, etc.)*
- *No children using the internet without volunteer/parent supervision*
- *No parents out after nine o'clock unless for work*
- *No pets, not even goldfish*
- *No bird feeders*
- *No backpacks left out front*
- *No skipping or trading chores*
- *No leaving a mess*
- *No being late on financial or housekeeping obligations*
- *No TV in Common Room after nine o'clock during the week*
- *No loud music, anywhere, ever*

- *No*
- *No*
- *No*
- *No*
- *No*
- *No*
- *No*
- *NO!*

Her eyes narrowed into little slits and she pinned them on me again. "These regulations are in place to assure your safety, Elizabeth, and so we, as a community, get along with one another within these walls."

I shrank away from her words. Mom reached over and squeezed my hand three times.

"Lizzie understands," she said.

Miss May settled her attention back on Mom and kept talking. A small air-conditioning unit at the other end of the room made a whirring sound as it spit cool air between the vents. I studied the trees outside the bay window. The trunks of the giant oaks were so big around, you could slice a dining room table right out of the middle. Thick limbs, heavy with green acorns, stretched from corner to corner over a dirt yard. There wasn't anything on the *Rules for Considerate Living* list about not climbing trees, but I would bet one of my plastic horses if I was caught sitting in one, a new line would be added to the bottom of that list.

Mom and Miss May were hunched over the clipboard, looking at some papers, when a dog ran from behind the trunk of one of the trees. It stopped in the yard and stared at me through the window, her reddish-brown floppy ears raised slightly, like she was asking for something. Other than the ears, her body was solid white. She was so skinny, I could practically count her ribs. Her hips stuck out to a point on each side, stretching the skin tight, and a sagging, hairless belly looked like she must have a litter of puppies hidden somewhere. Just as quickly as she appeared, she darted off across the driveway and vanished into the woods.

Finally, Mom stood up and touched me lightly on the shoulder.

"We're done," she said.

Miss May led us down a long, low-ceilinged hall, rattling something about how the house was built when the human race was an average of two inches shorter than we are now, which accounted for the low ceilings and narrow hallways. The space Mom and I were going to share was a skinny room with a set of bunk beds on the right, a closet on the left, a small white dresser in a corner, and one metal folding chair. It was so cramped, we couldn't walk past the bunk beds at the same time without sliding sideways.

After we made two trips to bring in our suitcases and boxes, I pulled curtains away from a single window that was smaller than the flat-screen TV in my old bedroom. Outside, a skinny strip of yard was bordered by so many trees, it was mostly dirt for lack of sunshine. My life was shrinking inch by inch by inch.

Mom unzipped one of the suitcases and tried to stuff an armful of clothes into one drawer of the dresser, then tried another, her forehead bunched up tight like she was trying to solve a puzzle. The dresser would have been the right size for the playhouse I had when I was six.

"Did you see that dog in the yard when we were talking to Miss May?" I asked.

"No, I didn't."

"I think she has puppies somewhere."

She crammed a stack of my T-shirts into a drawer and shoved it closed with her hip, then unzipped the next suitcase. "Oh, that's nice."

"Why can't we hang the bird feeder? There are so many trees; there's even a red maple."

"I'm not sure," she said. "Miss May is very exacting, so I am sure she has a calculated reason for it."

I didn't even have to look up the word *exacting* to understand what Mom meant. She meant that Miss May was strict, and we weren't going to question her rules, even if we didn't understand them.

Looking at the world through the panes of the tiny window made me remember how Mom described what it was like visiting Dad in jail, where they had to talk to each other on a phone in a booth separated by glass. Neither of them wanted me to see him that way.

"Mom?"

"Hmmm?"

"Did you always think Dad did it, that he stole from his company?"

She stopped unpacking for a second. Her expression softened for the first time since she'd told me we were leaving home.

"I suspected something funny was going on, but no, it never occurred to me it was that."

"MaryBeth said it was called embezzling. She said I probably knew the whole time."

Mom ruffled my hair, then turned back to the business of unpacking. "You know, sweetie, what Dad did wasn't your fault or my fault. It was his fault. So let's just move forward and not think about it, okay?"

I scanned the woods outside again, looking for some sign of the dog, and wondering how I was supposed to "just move forward." How was I supposed to not think about my own father being in jail?

I wrote my first real poem that night. At least, I think it was real. If nothing else, it was a string of words I'd put together that expressed what I was feeling inside. That was my best understanding of how poetry worked.

Mom and I were in bed before dark. It was the first time I'd ever ended a day hungry, but neither of us wanted to go to the dining hall with all the other "families in transition." Instead, we split a package of graham crackers and two fruit cups we'd brought from home, drank tap water out of tiny paper cups we found in the bathroom, and crawled into our bunk beds under scratchy blankets and sheets so thin you could see through them. Every time Mom tossed or turned below me, the top bunk squeaked and rocked like it was waiting for one big movement to crash to the ground. She pushed her covers off, then pulled them back up, and sniffled so loud I could hear her over the whir of a tiny white fan Miss May lent us when we found out there was no air-conditioning in our room.

In what was left of the silver light trying to break through the murky glass of the window at the end of the room, I opened my diary and spilled my feelings onto the page. When I was done, I tucked the diary into the crevice between the side of my bunk and the wall, laid my head on a foam pillow, and tried not to think about anything at all.

"Mom?"

No answer.

"Mom?"

"Yes?"

"I have to go to the bathroom."

"Okay, you know where it is."

"It's dark."

I'm afraid.

The bed jiggled when Mom sat up. I held the side rail, which was supposed to keep me from falling to the floor.

"I'll go with you," she said.

Step by step, I climbed gingerly down the ladder, gripping each rung with my bare toes. Mom shined the flashlight on her cell phone in front of us and we went down the hall to our tiny bathroom. The trash can was full of something rank.

"What's that smell?" I whispered.

Mom lifted the lid, then slammed it shut. "Dirty diapers."

"Are we sharing this bathroom with someone else?"

"Apparently." She said it so quietly I almost couldn't hear. "It will be okay, Lizzie. We're only here until we are back on our feet. I promise."

Her voice cracked on "promise." She pulled me to her and laid my head on her shoulder. We stood like that, locked together, in our bare feet on that cold tile floor in the dark, and we wept.

THREE

The next day, Miss May organized a meet and greet for us to get to know the other families before Sunday dinner.

"Do I have to go?" I asked Mom.

"Yes, it's for us."

"We're not even going to be here that long. I don't know why we have to meet the other people."

We'd been alone at breakfast, which was instant oatmeal and juice boxes. It hardly filled my stomach, but at least the juice was grape.

"Regardless of how long we're here, we have to go."

"Do those people know?"

"Know what?"

"About Dad? What he did?"

"No one knows anything except that we are going through hard times and need a place to live until we are back on our feet. That's all."

"Well, I still don't see why we should have a happy, jolly get-together. It's not like we're all on a cruise ship together. It feels like a lie."

Mom sighed but said nothing. We sat on our beds for the rest of the day, reading, thinking, trying not to think, and waiting. I'd gotten used to being alone most of the time, ever since MaryBeth had her temper tantrum at school and everyone in the universe stopped talking to me. But at least before I was still at home. I had a TV in my bedroom and movies to watch. I could lie on the couch in the living room and read or sit at the kitchen table and draw. I even went outside to the privacy of our backyard and leaned against the trunk of the red maple tree to write in my diary. Plus, back home we'd had a car to go places. Here, it was just me and Mom, a set of bunk beds and a too-small dresser in a skinny room, with both of us trying to pretend it wasn't weird at all. But it was.

The meet and greet wasn't as bad as I expected. I stood with my back to the wall while most of the people nodded at Mom and told her their names. None of the other kids were the least bit interested in me, which was a relief. I knew they had to be wondering why we ended up at Good Hope, because I was wondering the same thing about them. But no one asked. No one seemed to care about much more than their dinner. Well, except a harried-looking, redheaded lady who was the last to come in, with a baby in her arms and two other little girls beside her. She wrestled them over to where we were standing in a corner by the coffeepot, half smiling, half grimacing.

"Hi, I'm Angela," she said, "and this is Hope." A little girl with dark hair tried to wriggle out of Angela's grasp. "Hope is four, going on seventeen. She doesn't like to be confined. She'd run off to the library by herself every day if I let her."

"Library?" Mom raised her eyebrows.

Angela plunked Hope into a folding chair and pushed it up to the table.

"Yeah. Down the path behind the house," she said. "You can get a card if you like to read."

Mom wrapped her arm around my shoulders and gave a little squeeze. "We're big readers, both of us."

"Me too," Angela said. "Without a book, don't know how I'd make it through sometimes."

She grabbed another squirming girl and turned her around to us. This one scrunched her face and whined, "No-no-no-no-no!"

"This is Faith. She's two—going on two, in case you can't tell."

Faith pulled away and scrambled under the table. Angela shook a finger at her.

"Manners, Faith. Remember our manners."

Faith shook her finger back.

Angela rolled her eyes, then picked up a baby from the floor and kissed the pile of brown curls on top of her head.

"And this is my mopsy-bunny, Charity."

Charity had fat, rosy cheeks and clear blue eyes that reminded me of the porcelain doll collection my grandma had had in her house when I was little. The baby bounced in her mother's arms, then leaned forward and reached plump hands out to me.

"Awwwww, look at that," Mom said.

"You want to hold her?"

"I mean, I haven't held a lot of babies before—"

Angela didn't wait for me to finish. She deposited the baby in my arms just as a series of *putt-putt* sounds came from inside her diaper. Charity giggled and wrapped her fingers in my hair, then laid her cheek on my shoulder and purred like a kitten.

"My sweet baby," Angela said, stroking Charity's face. "Making the world a happier place one smile at a time."

The only other people we had any kind of conversation with were a lady in a wheelchair, Mrs. Ivanov, and her son, Leonard, who translated everything for her. Whenever Mrs. Ivanov wanted Leonard to speak for her, she tugged on his shirt, and he folded his lanky body at the waist to get close enough to hear her tiny voice.

"Skazhite im, chto vy khodite v srednyuyu shkolu," she said.

Leonard stood up but didn't look up. He stared at his shoes—or maybe my shoes.

"My mother says to tell you I go to high school," he said. His words had sharp edges to them.

"That's nice, Leonard," Mom said. "Do you like it?"

He shrugged, still focused on the floor. Mrs. Ivanov tugged on his shirt again.

"Skazhi devushke, chto my mozhem byt' druz'yami," she said.

"My mother says you can be friends," Leonard told the floor.

"How nice," Mom said. "We'd like that."

Leonard leaned down again and said something to Mrs. Ivanov. "My dolzhny poyti obedat' seychas."

She patted his hand, then waved to Mom.

"We must go to dinner now," Leonard said. He shot a dark look at me, then wheeled his mother away and settled her at one of the tables. A line of people had formed at a long counter where our dinner was set out in big ceramic bowls.

Mom squeezed her hands together. "Well, that was painless, right?"

"I guess," I said. "Where are all these people from?"

"I don't know, and it's none of our business. We're all here because we are in a tricky spot in our lives. That's all anyone needs to know."

My nerves jittered when we sat down to dinner. It had been only me and Mom for so long; the noise of seven families eating together made me want to run back to our room. But I was hungry, so I stayed.

First thing Monday, Mom and I found the path behind the house and went in search of the library. About five minutes along, a narrow, less-worn trail veered off to the right and disappeared around a bend.

"Which way?" I asked.

"Angela said to stay left."

So we went left.

The library was much smaller than the one in our old town, and it was inside a house. Upstairs, on the second floor, was a whole separate store that had nothing to do with the library. Mom and I went to the desk to get new cards.

"Do you have proof of residency?" asked the lady at the desk.

Mom handed her a folder of papers.

"What's that?" I asked.

"From Miss May," Mom said. "They verify our address."

My face heated up. I waited for the lady to say something, but she just kept typing, then handed the papers back to Mom without even looking at us.

"Got it," she said. "You're all set."

After we each picked out two books, Mom wanted to go upstairs and scout out the second floor.

"Oh, it's a consignment shop," she said when we got to the top.

"What does that mean?"

"They sell things someone else didn't need anymore."

She pulled a few pairs of jeans off the racks and checked the handwritten price tags.

"Wow, these are your size and they're only five dollars."

"Mom, no, they were some stranger's first," I said.

"There is absolutely nothing wrong with that. Didn't you share clothes with MaryBeth? Anyway, this shop will be good to keep in mind when you outgrow what you have now."

We didn't buy anything, but on the way to the stairs I spied a corner full of horse-riding stuff. Paddock boots, beige and brown riding breeches, used crops, and one single black velvet riding helmet exactly like the one in the mudroom back home. I forced myself away and caught up with Mom downstairs. No need to torture myself with reminders of everything we'd left behind.

During our first couple of weeks at Good Hope, Mom and I walked the path to the library every day, even if we hadn't finished the books we'd checked out. We liked being there. It was cool and quiet, with room to move around and comfy chairs to read in. Mom made friends with Linda, the lady who worked at the checkout counter and, if there wasn't a line when we went in, Mom would sit with her and talk while I found a place to read. A few times, I even heard Mom laugh again.

On our way back to Good Hope, we liked to stop where the trail split and the trees thinned enough to let sunlight warm the honeysuckle vines, releasing the intoxicating fragrance into the air.

"Our very own honeysuckle spa," Mom said.

We sat on a fallen tree trunk and read a little more, or I'd get out the pink diary and jot down descriptive nature words to keep for poems I wanted to write.

One afternoon we were meandering along the trail when Mom pointed up ahead.

"Look, Lizzie!"

The mother dog I'd seen on our first day was racing away from the back of the house, gripping a brown plastic bag in her teeth. Pieces of trash spilled from a rip in the side.

"That's the dog I told you about!"

The dog stopped when she saw me and Mom, dropped the bag, then clamped her jaws around it again and darted off between the trees.

"She's so skinny," Mom said.

"Didn't it look like she had puppies somewhere?"

"She's probably trying to find food for them, poor thing."

"Do you think Miss May would let me give her leftovers from our meals?"

We were just coming around the bend at the back of the house when I said that. Miss May was bent over by the trash bins, picking up litter spread all around a can that had tipped on its side.

"Varmints," she grumbled. "Nasty, no good, lazy varmints."

"There's your answer, I'm afraid," Mom said.

That night Miss May posted a notice on the bulletin board in the dining hall.

DO NOT LEAVE TRASH CAN LID OPEN!
STRAY ANIMALS ARE GETTING
INTO THE TRASH AGAIN.
ALWAYS LOCK THE LID
AFTER DUMPING BAGS.

After dinner, I crawled to my bunk to write about the dog. Mom left me alone and went to the common room, only to come back a few minutes later, her eyes lit up.

"Guess what? It's game night," she said from the doorway. "They're going to play Monopoly, and we're invited!"

"Are you going?"

"Why would I not? Come with me. It'll be fun."

"No, Mom, please, I can't."

She stepped inside and closed the door behind her. "Why can't you?"

I turned to face the wall. "I just don't want to, not with all those people."

"It's fewer people than we eat dinner with every night."

I shrugged in answer. That was kind of the point. It was easier to keep my distance in a crowd. She reached across my bunk and gently rubbed my back.

"Will you do this for me?" she asked.

Her voice was so sad, I couldn't say no. Slowly, I climbed down from my bunk and followed her to the common room. A round table, covered with a green cloth, and some metal folding chairs had been set up in the middle of the room. Leonard glanced up from dividing the money, then looked away quickly. I couldn't tell for sure, but it's possible he rolled his eyes when he muttered something to his mother in Russian.

Mrs. Ivanov's chin barely reached over the top of the table, but her smile filled the whole room. She patted the chair beside her, motioning for Mom to sit.

"Thank you."

"Spasibo."

"You both say thank you," Leonard said absently. His attention was still on doling out the play money.

A man named Brad, who had sat with me and Mom a couple of times at dinner, came in with his twin boys, David and Daniel. I'd never seen those boys when they weren't tormenting each other. David shoved his brother and reached across the table for the plastic cup of tokens.

"I pick first!" he snarled.

Daniel shoved back. "You always pick first!"

"Boys, stop!" Brad said sharply. Then he sighed. Brad was always sighing. "Unless anyone else objects, David will pick the first token, and Daniel, you can take the cup around for others to choose theirs. Everybody all right with that?"

No one cared. David made a face at his brother, then picked out the miniature cannon. Daniel made his way around the table with the plastic cup. Mom took the iron, Mrs. Ivanov took the thimble, and I dug out the little Toto dog from the bottom. The dice were rolled and our first game night at Good Hope began.

Ten minutes in, I drew the Get Out of Jail Free card. I stared at the glaring orange piece of cardboard burning in my hand, so hot I dropped it, faceup, right by Marvin Gardens. Everyone else waited for me to do something, like tuck it under the edge with my money, or speak, or anything. But I couldn't move.

Finally, Leonard picked it up and waved it around for everyone to see. His black eyes danced, and his lips were drawn into some kind of weird smile.

"Get out of jail free. You need that one. It is like gold, yes?"

"It was a coincidence, Lizzie," Mom said later. "Leonard doesn't know any more about us than we do about him."

"How do you know that for sure? How do we know Miss May didn't tell everyone before we came?"

Mom sat on her bed and tucked her hands between her knees. "We don't. But we have to have faith that these are good people who are trying to help us."

"You can have all the faith you want," I said, climbing up to my bunk. "Except for eating or going to the bathroom or out the door, I'm staying in this stupid room until we leave here forever."

FOUR

On a Wednesday morning, I snuck an extra piece of toast from breakfast into our room. I'd only seen the mother dog one other time, sniffing around the trash cans searching for food. Miss May saw her, too, and had run out the back door wielding a broom, screaming, until the dog bolted for the woods.

I propped open the window and leaned my elbows on the sill, waving the toast around in the hopes the dog would smell it. Mom startled me when she came back from the laundry room with a freshly ironed dress draped over her arm.

"What are you looking at out there?"

I let my arm dangle so she wouldn't see the toast.

"Just trying to find that dog. She's probably really hungry since the trash cans are locked now."

"Don't feed that dog, please. We don't need any trouble."

I let the toast drop to the ground and slid the window shut. "Where do you think that other path goes to?"

Mom dug shiny black shoes out of the closet, pulled a slip from a drawer, then stood in the middle of the floor looking lost.

"What path?"

"You know, where it veers off to the right when we go to the library."

"I don't know where it goes. Why?"

"Just wondering about the dog. Where are you going?"

She puckered her forehead. "Come here, sweetie. Let's talk for a minute."

"What is it? What's wrong?"

"Nothing is wrong. Come sit."

I sat next to her on the bed, so close our shoulders touched.

"I'm going to testify today," she said.

"Testify about Dad? Is this his trial?"

"Not yet. His lawyer asked me to come answer some questions."

"What kind of questions?"

"What I knew or didn't know about—well, about what Dad did." She fingered a gold button on the dress. "I'll only be gone a few hours."

"I'm going with you."

I jumped up and started throwing clothes together. She took them from me and shook her head. "You can't come. This is a grown-up thing."

"Yes, I can, and I'm going with you!"

I yanked the clothes from her and pulled jeans on over my pajama shorts. Mom stood in front of me, her blond hair already curled at the ends, her face pinched and sad.

"Lizzie, stop. I'm sorry you have to go through this—I'm sorry we *both* have to go through this—but I'm trying to do everything they ask so the court will release my bank account."

"What does that even mean?"

"It means that when Dad was arrested, the court froze our bank accounts so I couldn't use the money, even what came to me when Grandma and Granddad died. Once the court knows that money is mine and not Dad's, hopefully they'll let us have it back. I promise I'll only be gone a few hours."

"Why do we even have to do things like talk to lawyers?" I asked. "What did we do wrong?"

Mom pulled me to her and pressed my cheek against her shoulder. "Absolutely nothing, sweetie. You and I did not do anything wrong."

"Then why does it always feel that way?"

Half an hour later, a lady from the lawyer's office came to pick up Mom.

“Go spend the morning at the library,” Mom said. “I’ll be back shortly after lunch.”

As soon as the car pulled away from Good Hope, I ran to our room, grabbed my diary, and signed out in Miss May’s ledger, writing *LIBRARY* next to my name. I had no intention of going to the library. I was going to find that hungry dog and her puppies, and give her the toast I’d dropped out the window.

At the split in the trail, I stopped to catch my breath. It was my first time alone in the woods, and I liked the feeling of being on my own again. Fingering the waxy honeysuckle leaves, I thought of how the path between our old house and MaryBeth’s started and ended with this same kind of vine. I’d walked that path by myself since I was nine. This was really no different, except now someone else could be walking the old one. Maybe someone else already lived in our house, slept in my room, and gazed at the red maple outside the window where my grandparents’ ashes lay waiting for us to come home.

I placed the toast on the fallen trunk where Mom and I liked to stop, hoping the dog would find it, and sat down to write in my diary. No matter what Mom believed or tried to make me believe, I knew we would never be going back. Even after Dad’s trial, when he’d get out of jail, I didn’t really want to live in our old town, anyway. Not after all the people who were supposed to be our friends had treated Mom and me like criminals. No one rallied around us except Mrs. Alfieri, but that was only so she could collect gossip. Even my aunt Rebecca, Dad's sister in California, accused Mom of knowing the whole time what was going on and bringing shame to the family. After she said that on the phone, we never heard from her again.

After I'd written enough to feel a little better, I got up and moved along the trail veering away from the library, heading toward the unknown. I jogged around twists and turns, down little slopes, and up over ridges, jumping a thin, dry creek and landing on earth that was cushion soft under my sneakers. I kept going and going until the light in the woods began to change, the trees thinned, and the path ended behind the twisted trunk of a double chestnut.

On the other side of the tree, a small pony paddock stood empty. Tufts of grass grew in clumps under the rails of a rough wood fence. The land beyond it opened up to gentle fields dotted with ponies and horses along a hillside, their heads disappearing in lush emerald grass. A narrow dirt road cut straight between the fields, down a dip, then up and up and up until it ended at a big barn standing like a red castle at the top of a hill.

I tucked my diary into the V where the trunk of the chestnut split and stared at the horse farm. In the stillness of that summer morning, I heard only the faraway sounds of ponies' teeth ripping grass from the earth as they moved slowly across the hills. Sunlight bounced off their backs, sparkling like the brand-new copper penny had so long ago when I'd flipped it in the air above a water fountain and wished for a pony of my own.

I'd waited two years for the riding lesson that was supposed to happen last December. Once Dad was gone, no one ever said anything about it again. It wasn't important anymore. It wasn't *essential.* Even I didn't think about it, except for when the helmet had dropped in the closet that day and again when I'd seen the riding clothes at the thrift store. I never dared to imagine there would be ponies in my life until after Dad's trial, after we were back on our feet.

A tiny smile spread across my face. I'd never been so happy to be wrong. That one riding lesson might have been abandoned, but not the possibility of ponies. They were right here in front of me, at the end of an unknown trail.

By the time Mom got home, I'd used up the last pages of the pink diary writing the beginnings of a poem about what I'd found earlier and had resorted to cramming teeny, tiny letters along the edges of the paper. I didn't hear her come in until she closed the door and dropped her purse on the floor. The look on her face jerked me out of my beautiful pony-dream.

"What's wrong?"

She pressed her lips together, then started pacing from the window to the door and back again.

"Mom, you're scaring me. What happened?"

She stopped abruptly, her arms crossed, then sank onto the metal chair.

"He betrayed us," she said.

Her voice was sharp and hollow and frightened me. I climbed cautiously down the ladder and sat on the lower bunk.

"What do you mean?"

"Your dad is already out of jail."

"How did he get out?"

"Someone else had money and paid his bail. He's been out for a month."

"A month?"

My mind swirled, trying to put pieces of this news together. Dad was out of jail. I counted back. He'd been out when Mom and I moved to Good Hope, and we were still here. All these weeks and he hadn't come to see me. Mom slumped forward, rested her elbows on her knees, and let her head hang.

"I can't believe I'm left to tell you this. It should be him."

"Tell me what?"

She shook her head so her hair swung in front of her face.

"Give me your phone," I said. "I'll call him."

"You can't call him. He doesn't have his old phone anymore."

"Well, what phone does he have, then? Give me the number."

"Stop, Lizzie," she pleaded. "Just stop."

The air between us stilled. She stood up and got her pajamas from the drawer. It wasn't even two o'clock in the afternoon and she was going to bed.

"Mom, this isn't fair. You have to tell me."

"He's out, Lizzie. His trial isn't for another few months, but we are staying here. We'll just keep waiting to see what happens."

"Where is he?"

"He's not at the old house, if that's what you mean."

"No, it isn't. I mean, why isn't he here with us?"

She took her toothbrush bag and left the room. I heard the water turn on in the bathroom sink, then shut off. A minute later she came back. Her face was red like she'd scrubbed off her makeup too hard with a really rough washcloth.

"Move over, sweetie. I need to lie down for a nap. It's been a long day."

I moved to the chair. She pulled the covers up around her shoulders and closed her eyes.

"Mom," I said. "I need to know."

"I know you do," she whispered.

I waited for what seemed like an eternity, my heart racing. Finally, she stuck her hand out from under the covers and took mine.

"He isn't coming to get us, Lizzie. We aren't going home. The only reason he had the money to get out is because of a woman he knew before. She paid fifty thousand dollars to get him out. He's staying with her."

"Who is it? And why does that mean he has to stay with her?"

She squeezed her eyes tight and spread her fingers wide. Her wedding ring was gone. "It means he chose her instead of us. Because she could get him out of jail and we couldn't."

Everything went silent again as the truth about my dad dirtied the air. He was living with some rich lady while Mom and I were at Good Hope. He hadn't even cared enough to help, or come see me. He'd sold us out.

My heart splintered into a thousand pieces.

FIVE

On a hot, sticky Monday, exactly one month after we'd left our old home, Mom went off to work at a job for the first time since I was born.

"It's at an architectural company," she said, brushing mascara onto her lashes in the mirror. "Having a good job will get us into our own home a lot faster."

I was sitting in my usual place by the window, watching for any sign of the hungry dog. "If Dad got money from that lady, why doesn't he pay for us to get out of here?"

At first, I'd been devastated by his betrayal. The worst

part was that I missed him all over again, as much as I had when he first left. But it took only a few days to get over that. He hadn't even tried to make our lives easier. That made me feel unwanted. Discarded. Chased off. Like the dog.

"That's an excellent question," Mom said. "But it's one I don't have an answer for."

"How long will it take for us to get our own place?"

"That depends on how fast I get the debts cleared up. We're allowed to stay here a year, and I'm ninety-nine percent sure I can make it in that length of time."

"A year? We're going to be here an entire year? That's one-twelfth of my life!"

Silence.

"I'm doing my best," she finally said.

"I know you are, Mom. I'm sorry."

Before she left, she tore out used pages from a spiral notebook the lawyer people had given her. "You can have this, sweetie. I don't need it anymore. First paycheck and I'll buy you some sketch pads, too."

She kissed the top of my head and went out the door to catch a bus to her new job.

That first morning, I returned two books to the library even though I hadn't read them yet. Linda was at the desk, fanning herself with a handful of papers.

"Hi, Lizzie. No Mom today?"

"No, she started a new job."

"Oh, that's right, good for her," she said. "Where is she working again?"

"For an architect."

"Nice. In an air-conditioned office building I bet. Our AC is out again."

"Yeah, it's warm in here."

"Tell me about it. So, what are you going to do with the rest of your summer?"

"I don't really know. I don't have any new friends yet."

Linda's eyebrows stitched together. She fanned herself faster, like my problem made her hotter.

"I was wondering," I said, "do you need volunteer help? Maybe I could come for a little bit each day, and I don't know, restock books or sweep or something?"

She stopped fanning and studied my face. "How old are you?"

"I'll be thirteen at the end of December. Right after Christmas."

"Hmmmm," she said. "It's a dilemma."

"A dilemma?"

"Yes. Typically you have to be fourteen to be a regular volunteer, for it to count toward community service hours for school."

"I don't really care about the community service hours."

"I can see that," she said. "Would your mom sign something saying she gave permission?"

"I'm sure she would!"

Linda got busy typing up a letter. When she was done, she read it over, made some kind of change, then printed it and handed it to me.

"Have her read and sign this. If she has any questions, she can call me."

"Thank you so much, Linda. I won't disappoint you."

I had successfully engineered a cover story for leaving Good Hope every day while Mom worked. A couple of hours at the library allowed me time at the horse farm with no one questioning where I'd been. I'd only been able to sneak over to see the horses twice since that first day, because I wasn't ready to share my secret and risk being told I wasn't allowed.

"I have no doubts at all," Linda said. I was halfway to the door when she stopped me. "Remind your mom we are supposed to go to the movies sometime. She can pick which one."

"I will and thank you!"

For what was left of the second hottest summer on record in Connecticut, I spent two hours every weekday at the library, straightening shelves, sweeping, and whatever else Linda needed done, including occasionally helping her finish her daily crossword puzzle. Sometimes we talked about my poems.

"I always wanted to be an English teacher," she said. "Specifically, I wanted to teach poetry. Who is your favorite poet?"

"I don't really have one yet," I said. "But I want to learn

how to write really good poems."

"The best way to learn about poetry is to read it."

Linda got up, disappeared in between shelves of periodicals, and came back a minute later with a pale green book in her hands.

"Robert Frost," she said. "Start reading his stuff. We'll move on from there."

The book was barely bigger than my hand and had a gold ribbon attached to the binding to bookmark the ivory pages.

"Thank you."

She smiled and settled into her seat like she was pleased with herself. "Maybe I'll get to do that teaching stint after all. You'll be my guinea pig."

Every day, the very second my two hours at the library were up, I took off down the trail to spy on the horse farm. I lay flat on my belly in the grass near the shaded edge of the woods and watched the horses' muscles ripple as they moved across the hills. I made up names for each of them and sketched pictures in the new spiral notebook Mom had given me, being careful to utilize every inch of space on each page. And I wrote poems. Really awful poems, mostly. But every once in a while, a string of lyrical words would appear, almost as if someone else wrote them. I read them out loud over and over, trying to understand why those in particular made music in my heart.

Mostly, I watched the horses and ponies. Sometimes one of them would spook and they would all take off, galloping side by side, up and down the hills. Their hooves pounded the earth, kicking up a cloud of dust that spun a smell in the air so thick and sweet, it followed me into my dreams. Every afternoon, at exactly the same time, I left the grassy area and hid under the cover of trees when two men walked down the hill to collect the horses from their fields and take them back to the barn. When the last horse was gone and the pastures empty, I gathered my writing tools and traipsed around to the far side of the farm where an old stone wall ran straight through a dense grove of trees, and I waited.

Between my hiding place and the back side of the barn was a small riding ring where a man named Joe and a girl called Kennedy took turns teaching kids how to ride. Just before four o'clock, a steady stream of cars pulled down the driveway and dropped off students wearing helmets and boots—nearly all of them girls. They'd disappear into the front of the barn, then come out to the ring a few minutes later, leading the same horses and ponies I'd watched running free in the fields not even an hour before. When the riders mounted their horses, I straddled the stone wall and pretended to slip my feet into silver stirrups. With an imaginary set of reins between my fingers, I imitated those riders trotting around the ring, going up and down, up and down, and dreamed of the day my hands would hold not just a book about ponies but a real mane, soft and feathery, twisted between my fingers.

I envied those girls with so much passion, my heart

churned into hate. I hated their matching pink shirts with *Birchwood Stables* embroidered on the back and their black helmets, so much like the one I'd left behind. I hated the way they high-fived each other after flying over the jumps Joe or Kennedy set for them. After the lessons were over, my jealousy peaked when I watched them feed peppermints from leather-gloved hands to the ponies I could only love from a distance with all my empty, homeless heart. And on the rare afternoons I let myself think about Dad on the walk home, I hated him, too.

AUTUMN

SIX

By the time school started in September, I already knew the names of a bunch of the kids from Birchwood who would be my classmates. I learned them from hearing the riders talk after the lessons, when they led the horses and ponies around the ring to cool them out. Usually they walked in pairs, but on Tuesdays and Thursdays there was a group of four girls about my age who rode together and walked their horses around the ring all in a row: Rikki, Sabrina, Jasmine, and Jade. One time, they walked so close to my hiding place, Jasmine saw me straddling the stone wall like it was a pony. She caught my eye through the trees and we stared at each other while she and her friends meandered past, then she looked away without saying anything.

The night before school began, I studied the bus map Mom gave me and found the next closest stop after ours. It was almost half a mile away, but I didn't care about the extra walking. It meant no one would see me getting on at Good Hope Lane. The shelter was the only house on the road and there was no need for anyone to know where I lived. That would only lead to questions about why we lived there, and my secret about what Dad had done wouldn't be a secret anymore.

I waited by myself on the opposite side of Brook Drive until I saw the yellow bus round a corner. Just before it squealed to a stop, I darted across to where everyone had lined up, and slipped into the empty seat behind the driver. I should have known he'd complain. Bus drivers are never happy until the last week of school.

"Hey," he said over his shoulder. "Don't run in front like that again, got it?"

"Yes, sorry."

"Lose my job if I run you over." He closed the door and the bus jerked forward, letting loose that loud *whoosh* noise.

A few minutes later, we pulled into a roundabout driveway at the school. The building looked pretty much the same as the middle school back home. There didn't seem to be anything remarkably different about the students either or the way they dressed—lots of jeans and Converse sneakers in assorted styles and colors. Mom had bought me a pair last year before name-brand sneakers were considered *unessential*. I'd had to yank and pull and practically bind my feet to get them on this year, and my toes were so squished they might never unkink again. But the struggle was worth it. If nothing else about me was the same as these other kids, at least my shoes were.

A boy with long blond hair was the last one off the bus ahead of mine. Apparently, he didn't care whether he looked the same as everyone else or not. He stopped on the curb and hooked his thumbs into a tooled leather belt—the kind with a giant silver buckle on the front—as if he wanted to be sure everyone saw it. Then he raised his chin a little and headed for the front door, scuffing the heels of shiny black cowboy boots against the concrete with each step. I wasn't the only one who noticed he stood out. Even the bus driver lowered his sunglasses to look.

Mom had told me to pick up my schedule in the office before class. I waited at a counter until a lady with purple cat-eye glasses came out of a cubicle. She pointed at me with long fingernails painted plum and tipped in silver, an exact color match to the Go Rockets! banner hanging on the wall.

"New student?"

I nodded.

She pointed past me. "You too?"

"Yes, ma'am."

It was the blond boy with the cowboy boots. I moved aside to make room for him.

"Last name?" the lady asked me.

"St. Clair."

"And you?"

"McDaid," the boy said.

"I'm Ms. Bacigalupi," she said, pointing to her badge. "Don't try to pronounce it. Just call me Miz Bee." She had a twinge of a Southern accent.

"Miz Bee?" I asked.

"Close enough for chocolate," she said.

Miz Bee opened a metal drawer, riffled through some files, and came back with two packets.

"Bryce McDaid, this is yours," she said, reading the label on the front. "All the way from Wyoming, huh? Schedule is inside. Elizabeth St. Clair, here is yours."

"Lizzie," I said.

Miz Bee eyeballed me over the cat-eye glasses and raised her brows like she thought I was being rude. "Excuse me?"

"Nothing, it's okay, I'm good, thank you so much." I turned quickly and fled into the hall.

It was easier than I'd feared to keep to myself. Most everyone else already knew one another, so no one bothered to try and talk to me except Bryce McDaid. That was only because we collided trying to go through the door to history class at the same time.

"Ah! Sorry!" I said.

"No worries." Bryce grinned and waved me ahead of him.

I spotted an empty desk in the back corner and sank into the seat, clutching my backpack in my arms. One more class until lunch. Then I could find a place to be alone and mentally regroup for the rest of the day.

Bryce stood by the next desk over. "You mind?"

"No," I said. "Go for it."

I unzipped my pack and pretended to search for something so I didn't have to make eye contact with anyone else in the room. That worked until a group of noisy girls came in, clinging to each other like a single unit of human-ness instead of four individual people. But they were four individuals. I knew this because they were the four girls who rode at Birchwood every Tuesday and Thursday afternoon. Before I could sink lower in my chair, Jasmine caught sight of me. Her dark eyes flashed, like she was trying to place where she'd seen me. Before she could recall, Jade jabbed her in the side.

"Look, Jasmine, it's that cute boy."

And just like that, all eyes were riveted on Bryce McDaid. He'd hooked the cowboy boots around the legs of his chair and was tipping it back and forth while he doodled in a notebook. His hair fell down over the left side of his face and eye, and he was completely unaware that everyone was staring. Not until class started, anyway, and the teacher, Coach Redmond, did what no kid ever wants a teacher to do.

"Ah, you ladies sitting in the group back there, let's focus on the work at hand and not the cute new boy."

Waves of giggles rippled across the room. Bryce's head flew up. He shot a quick look at the girls, then turned his chair so his back was to them and he faced me. His cheeks had gone from alabaster to pink to all-out crimson in just a few quick breaths.

When class was over and everyone else had left, he raised his eyebrows and grinned. "Glad that's done. You have lunch now?"

"Yeah."

"Good, me too. Let's go."

My thoughts of finding a place for solitude vanished. I fell in behind Bryce and we made our way through the crowded halls to the cafeteria. When it was my turn to pay, I held out three one-dollar bills. The lady at the register shook her head.

"We use the Payment Plus system here, hon."

"What does that mean?"

"It's a card. Should have come with your new student paperwork."

I opened my backpack and dug around in the folder until I found a purple plastic card with my name printed on the front.

"Is it this?"

"Yup, sure is." She swiped the card, then squinted at the computer screen. "No money in the account, though."

"Money?"

"Your guardian is supposed to put money in the account to pay for your lunch."

"Oh. I didn't know. Can I pay with the cash?"

"Noooo," she said, shaking her head. "We don't take cash. I'll get Mrs. Samuels to okay an IOU."

She reached for a button on a microphone, but before she could announce to the entire cafeteria full of seventh graders that I didn't have money to pay for my lunch, Bryce nudged me aside and held out his card.

"She can use mine," he said. "Put both mine and hers on it, please."

"You related? You have to be related to share cards."

"Cousins," he said, tapping my foot with the tip of his boot.

"Yeah, cousins," I echoed.

"Got it," the lunch lady said. "Cousins."

We found seats at the only empty table, which happened to be right next to the janitor's closet. The smell of ammonia wafted through the air. Bryce stared at his plate of what might have been meat loaf but looked more like dirty tissues that had gelled into a mold.

"Not sure which smells worse, the ammonia or the meat loaf."

That made me laugh. "Yeah, but at least lunch is a break from classes."

"True. You like history?"

"Pretty much. Better than math."

"Definitely better than math."

Bryce pushed the corner of his meat loaf with a fork. It bounced back like it was made from rubber. "Ugh."

I unwrapped my turkey sandwich and sighed. White bread, no mayo, no lettuce, no tomato, no pickle, and probably no salt.

"Looks boring," Bryce said. He opened a pocket of his backpack and pushed an almond-berry granola bar and a clementine across the table to me. "Here, fill in with this. It's not much, but at least you won't starve."

"Thanks."

He peeled a clementine with his thumb and dropped the rind onto the table. The citrus smell mingled with the ammonia in a surprisingly pleasant way.

"I always bring food from home," he said. "I'm a part-time vegetarian with an appetite. You can't count on school food to have enough options for people like me."

"Why did you get meat loaf if you're a vegetarian?"

He poked it again with his finger and grinned. "It looked humorous."

For the second time on a day when I did not expect to even smile, Bryce had made me laugh. By the time lunch was over, he felt like a longtime friend. And he hadn't asked about where I lived or anything about my family. Not once.

My last class of the day was English, which I decided was the reward for fumbling through everything from history and math to PE. Ms. Fitzgerald's classroom popped with personality. Volumes of Shakespeare and Harry Potter were stacked along the windowsills, along with other classics and fantasy books. There was a pointy pink-and-green cactus on her desk and a purple orchid with sprays of blooms draping between collections of poetry books on shelves. Colorful rugs with rope fringe were tacked up on the walls, and Ms. Fitzgerald had pinned handwritten poems to each one. Different-colored plastic beanbag chairs on the floor were stenciled with "Reading is Rad" or "The Wonder of Words" and "Drop Everything and Read." She also had an aquarium full of neons and angelfish.

Ms. Fitzgerald didn't look like a regular teacher, either. Her jeans had faded patches on the knees, and her sandals looked like they'd made a cross-country trek at least twice. A dozen black braids fell almost to her waist, and each one had a tiny wooden bead fastened on to the end. When she walked between the desks, looking left and right to make eye contact with her new students, she let her braids swing, and the beads clicked like miniature castanets. One of the first things out of her mouth was about poetry.

"Every day we will read a poem out loud," she said.

She stopped beside my desk and smiled, like she already knew I was a poetry kid.

"It doesn't matter if we're working on a poetry segment or not," she said, moving on. "One of you will read out loud, right up here in front of the class."

She paused, listening to the shuffle of students wiggling

in their chairs, then lifted a thick, worn leather book from the corner of her desk and unlaced two leather straps that were wrapped around to tie it shut.

"You can tell which poems are favorites," she said, flipping through the pages and showing us raggedy edges. "This may feel uncomfortable in the beginning, but it is going to help you expand your horizons. Force you out of your comfort zone."

She scanned the room. Her eyes settled on me again, and her lips turned up in a small smile.

"You're safe in my class," she said quietly, as if she was saying it only to me. "No one is going to judge you."

SEVEN

It took the whole first month of school before I felt ready to read a poem in front of the class. I couldn't bear the idea of standing up there, red-faced and fumbling over words in the big leather book like a lot of the other people did when it was their first time. Linda said I should pick one of my favorites, something I already knew by heart, so I chose "Stopping by Woods on a Snowy Evening," written by Robert Frost.

Mr. Frost had lived in the same Vermont town where my grandparents grew up. Even though he died a long time ago, that made me feel like I knew him personally. I'd seen his cabin where he wrote a lot of his poems and imagined him sitting by a snapping fire at night, with snow falling outside frosty windows, scribbling his day's thoughts onto yellow paper where they appeared in lovely, perfect form. Words that made my heart ache for a less complicated life.

On my poem-reading day, I got through it in one piece, even though I almost choked when I read the part that made me think of Dad's betrayal—the lines about promises to keep. The class clapped for me like they did for everyone else, and when I looked around, I realized I knew the names of only a few of the students. Privately, I had vowed to get through the year without being invited to someone's house after school—someone who wanted to be a friend and who might expect a return invitation. Friends asked questions. If these people knew about Dad's crime, they might judge Mom and me the way people back home had—as if we were the guilty ones, too.

There was a girl in my English class, Jenna, who I might have been friends with but changed my mind the day she read her poem out loud. Jenna was bouncy and energetic and had masses of rust-colored freckles across her nose. She sat next to me and talked a mile a minute, not really caring if I was listening or not. Jenna talked about Jenna, which was good for me but was annoying enough that the other kids steered clear of her.

On the day she read her poem, a couple of weeks after me, she didn't just read it; she performed it, like she was onstage.

She waved her hand through the air and swayed side to side, oblivious to the snickers rippling through the room and the boy in the back, Danny, silently imitating her gestures. Jenna's voice rose and fell dramatically when she moved from one stanza to the next. By the time she read the last line, her eyes were damp and she was out of breath. Two beats of silence went by before Ms. Fitzgerald spoke, two beats in which the rest of the class waited awkwardly, not sure if we were supposed to just applaud or give a standing ovation for such a performance.

"Beautifully done, Jenna," Ms. Fitzgerald finally said. She had moved next to Danny, who now sat obediently with his hands folded on his desk. "You might consider a career onstage someday. But you didn't tell us the name of the poem or why you chose it."

"Oh, right," Jenna said.

She licked her lips, lifted her shoulders, and smiled at me, like my approval meant everything. "It's titled, 'Invictus,' by William Ernest Henley, and I picked it because it was the poem that helped Nelson Mandela survive during his twenty-seven years in prison."

"An excellent choice. Thank you," Ms. Fitzgerald said.

She went on to talk about some kind of project the class was going to be starting soon, but "twenty-seven years in prison" pounded in my ears like a drumbeat. I didn't even know how long Dad would have to go to prison if he lost his trial, and right that second, I couldn't remember what Nelson Mandela had done that sent him away for so long.

Jenna smiled all the way back to her desk and whispered, "Thanks for the encouragement. I couldn't have gotten through it without you."

I had no idea what encouragement she was talking about. I shrugged and focused on scribbling nonsense on a piece of paper, pressing my pencil so hard the tip broke off and flew to the floor. Jenna leaned down and picked it up.

"Here you go," she said. "I have an extra." She handed me a pink pencil with cartoon unicorns all over it.

Ms. Fitzgerald strolled between rows of desks, still talking about something called the Partners in Poetry Project. "Think about whom you'd like to work with," she said, "and I would recommend choosing someone whose strengths will enhance areas in which you might need a boost. Perhaps one of you wants to write the poem and the other would create the visual aid."

Jenna touched my elbow with the eraser of her own unicorn pencil.

"Hey, want to be partners? You could come to my house one time to work on it, then I could go to yours, and we could switch like that. It would be fun. Want to?"

I shook my head. "No, but thanks."

"Really?" she squeaked. "You know I'm the only other one in this class who even cares about poetry, right?"

"I can't answer right this second," I said.

She paused just long enough for me to know she was surprised.

"Okay, well, think about it. We'd have fun, I guarantee you. And if you'd rather work at your house, that's okay with me. Either house is fine. Yours is probably more fun because my parents work all the time. I mean: All. The. Time!"

"Can we talk about it another day?"

Jenna's face fell. "Sure, no prob."

But I could tell it was a problem because she wouldn't look at me for the rest of class. Finally, the bell rang and everyone, including Jenna, bolted out the door. I sat in my seat, twirling the unicorn pencil until the room was empty, then walked to the front and stood by Ms. Fitzgerald's desk. My fingers drifted to the soft, faded leather of the poetry book.

"Hey, Lizzie, what's up?"

"Um, I know there's an odd number of students in this class, so I'd like to volunteer to work on the poetry project alone."

"Hmmmm," she said, studying me. She sat cross-legged in her chair, tapping a pencil against her knee. "You know, Lizzie, I feel like this is a difficult year for you for whatever reason. I'm not asking you to share anything personal, but maybe it would be good for you to be part of a team so you can connect with another student."

I wasn't prepared for her to try and talk me out of it, so I stalled by untying, then retying the leather strings around the poetry book.

"I'm just better working on my own," I mumbled.

She looked at me, and I looked at her, and I knew whoever spoke first was going to give in, so I dropped my eyes. It was impossible to explain.

"Could you work in a group of three?" she asked. "Would that be better?"

I shook my head. "Please, I'd really rather do it alone."

Finally, she smiled kind of sadly, then wrote something in the margin of her big lesson planner.

"Okay, then," she said. "Lizzie St. Clair, flying solo."

Flying solo. That was me.

The first afternoon I slipped out the back door of Good Hope and could actually see a smudge of the red barn through the trees, I knew something was different. Not because some of the leaves were finally giving way to the changing seasons and lay scattered on the ground, but because the closer I got to the horse farm, the more clearly I could hear Joe's voice piercing through the woods, sharp and alarming.

"Whoa, pony, whoa!" he yelled.

I dodged through the woods, hiding behind one tree after the next, my heart beating so hard it pulsed against the fabric of my turtleneck. Joe must have been near the end of the lane for me to hear him so clearly. Caution said for me to wait until he was gone, but the sounds of scuffling boots and hooves, and of a metal gate slamming against a wooden post, kept me moving forward until I got behind the double chestnut tree. Peering between the two trunks, I had a clear view of the closest paddock.

Joe stood in the corner, his face tilted forward, his arms clasping the head of a red pony. "Easy, little fella, easy now," he said, his voice calm and steady again.

Dust filtered down around them, coating Joe's shirt like flour did to Mom's hands when she used to bake, back when we had our own kitchen. The pony's body was pressed firmly against the wooden fence. His creamy white tail twitched left and right, left and right, and his sides heaved with each breath. Joe cradled the pony's head tightly against his own chest and rubbed a hand along the thick neck.

"Hush, little fella," he said. "Don't be afraid. This is your new home."

After a few minutes of soothing talk and stroking his neck and shoulder, Joe unbuckled the halter and backed away, then moved calmly to the gate. He hung the halter on the post and trudged away up the hill. The pony's head was raised on an arched neck, and his eyes stared toward the barn. He was frightened—and so beautiful the back of my knees went weak. I lowered myself to the ground and settled onto a pile of crisp leaves.

The pony's ear flicked back at the noise. He flung his body around and glared at me through the trees, then blew a loud snort and stamped one hoof into the dirt. My breath caught. I simply could not look away. His face was the same mahogany red as the rest of his body. Dark, smoldering eyes watched me from under a silky, custard-colored forelock draping half-way down his face. His legs were braced, his body poised, and his tiny black-tipped ears curved forward.

In that brief instant, when the pony and I stared at each other, I knew he'd been taken from someplace he'd known as home. I recognized the look in his eye that said he didn't understand, he didn't know where he was, and my own troubled heart shared his burden. We were alike, this pony and I. We were kindred spirits. Something magnificent rose inside me—something poetic yet so real I could almost feel the weight of it in my hands, and I thought instantly of Mr. Frost's poem "Fire and Ice."

"Fire," I whispered. "That's your name. Fire."

The magic was stolen by the sound of the men coming to collect the other horses from their fields. Fire whirled around and whinnied frantically as each horse was led away to the barn. Not one of them answered his call. When the last field was empty and he was the only horse left outside, Fire reared high, striking the air with both front hooves, then bolted across the paddock like a wild mustang. I crawled through dried grass to get closer and watched his muscles gather and stretch with each stride. His mane and tail streamed behind him, like flames licking the air. Just before colliding with the fence, he jammed his hooves into the dirt and skidded to a stop, his head held high and proud. Scanning the fields again, he hurled another call across the hills, this one still answered by silence.

My fingers touched the smooth skin of a small apple in my pocket. Wiping it shiny with my sleeve, I said his new name out loud.

"Fire!"

He startled and spun, spewing dust in a cloud around him. I waited for him to settle, then rolled the apple toward him in the dirt. His neck arched and he snorted, wide-eyed, sniffing when the apple stopped a few feet from his hooves. Without taking a bite, he studied me again with a look that seemed to say my companionship meant more to him than the offer of fruit. My whole heart melted.

By the time the lessons started on the far side of the barn, Fire had eaten both the apple and its core. He wandered from one side of the enclosure to the other, sniffing and exploring, and took a long drink from a trough of fresh water. Finally, he settled in and munched on the large flake of hay left for him by the shed. My mind was spinning with words and my heart was so full of new feelings, I knew I needed to capture them on paper, to make them mine forever.

"I have to go home, Fire," I said, "but I'll be back tomorrow. Promise."

His ears flicked at my voice, but he kept his head down in

the hay. I sprinted away, running back through the woods, thinking of Fire's eyes in that instant we became friends and of all the words waiting to be brought to life on the pages of my notebook. Nearing the fork in the trail, I heard him whinny again, and I smiled. This time, I knew he was calling for me.

EIGHT

The next day in school, Ms. Fitzgerald caught me drawing pictures of Fire in the margin of my poetry notebook. I was supposed to be compiling a list of active verbs, but my mind was at Birchwood with Fire. She tapped the best drawing, the one where Fire was looking right at me.

"Beautiful poetry comes from the feelings I sense in your drawings."

I covered the paper with my forearm. "Sorry. I guess I'm not in a list mood."

"Yes, but what is poetry if not the use of beautiful words

to express the feelings I see there? That's all I'm asking for. Beautiful words."

After school I checked in with Miss May, signed the new sheet, took a few mini carrots from the snack tray for Fire, then signed out again.

Library, I wrote.

Lie, I thought.

Since school had started, I was helping Linda at the library only a couple of hours during the week and most Saturday afternoons. Miss May didn't know that, though, and Mom had never outright asked. I made sure Linda saw me enough so no red flag would alert her to say anything to Mom, but so I still got plenty of horse-farm time.

I raced out the door and ran along the now familiar path toward Birchwood. As I got closer, I started listening for sounds that would reassure me Fire was still there. All day long I'd been worried he would be moved into the barn while I was at school. Then I'd have to figure out some other way to see him. That's where my brain had locked up. Unless he was in the little paddock by the woods, I had no plan.

Just before the chestnut tree, I jolted to a stop. Fire was still there, but he wasn't alone. Four girls were perched along the top rail of the fence, all of them wearing matching pink jackets—the kind with *Birchwood Stables* embroidered across the back. Jackets that said they belonged. Jackets I'd seen a thousand times, coveted a million, and silently wept over in my bunk above Mom.

It was Rikki, Sabrina, Jasmine, and Jade from history class, and from the Tuesday and Thursday group lessons. I quickly moved into the shadows and stifled a gasp. In all my mental ramblings during the day, in all my worries and fantasies and dreams and imaginings, not once had I considered that Fire might already belong to someone else.

Other than flattening his ears when one of the girls laughed too loud, Fire ignored them, his head down in a pile of hay. But something was different. Something had happened while I was gone. The afternoon before, his coat had shined like polished wood. Today, a layer of crusted dirt clung to his hairs. Streaks of dried sweat trailed down his legs, and his silky, cream-colored tail now hung in thick clumps—dark yellow and brown. Flecks of dust lingered in the silty afternoon sunlight.

"Look how adorable he is," Rikki said.

"Too bad he's too small for you to ride, Miss Basketball Star," Jasmine said, pointing to Rikki's long legs.

Sabrina flipped red braids over her shoulders. "He's not too small for me, and he's flashy, girls. Show-pony flashy and nothing less."

She jumped down from the fence. Fire's head jerked up when her feet hit the ground.

"Hey, pony, look, I have a treat," Sabrina said, holding out her hand.

She took a step closer and Fire spooked, pinning himself into the corner. He flipped his tail and swung his head, teeth bared, in her direction.

"You shouldn't be in there," Jade said.

"I'm fine," Sabrina answered. "I just want to pet him."

Fire flattened his ears and cocked a back hoof like he was ready to take out her kneecap with a swift kick. Sabrina inched forward.

"Hi, little pony," she said.

"Hey!" Behind the girls, Joe walked up beside a man I'd never seen before. "Get out of there!"

Sabrina jumped, then scrambled between the fence rails. "I'm sorry, Joe. I kind of just fell into the paddock, I didn't mean—"

"You know the rules about new horses," he said. "Leave them alone."

"Yes, I do. We all know. I'm sorry," she said.

"We didn't mean anything bad," Jasmine said.

The other man stood apart from Joe, his hands stuffed into his jacket pockets, his face grim.

"Hi, Mike," Rikki said to him in a fake-polite voice.

Mike nodded. "Rikki."

Joe jerked his head toward the barn. "Go on, get ready for your lesson. Mike and I have things to discuss."

"Who owns the new pony?" Jasmine asked.

"Did you not hear me? Go, please."

Rikki looped one arm through Sabrina's. "Okay, okay, we're going," she said.

The four of them pretended to canter away, the black letters on their pink jackets bobbing all the way up the lane. A stray leaf swept through the air over Fire, fluttering to the field beyond his paddock. I watched it twirl and float, its rusty color dancing against a sapphire sky, and wished my heart could float the same way. Then, maybe, I wouldn't feel so alone when I watched those four friends together.

Mike and Joe propped their arms along the top rail of the fence and studied Fire.

"He'll make a fancy show pony," Joe said.

Mike scowled. "I still don't understand why you spent my money to buy an untrained pony. It'll be months before he's ready to show, let alone sell."

"I know, but he came through the sale and there was just something about him—"

Mike flipped his hand like he was shooing away a fly. "Go on with your soft-heart stuff. We've had this conversation too many times. This is a business, Joe. Think like a businessman. Profit and loss. How much do you think you can get for him?"

"Once he's finished training, a couple of thousand. But if someone wants him when he's still green, a thousand, easy."

Mike smacked his palm against the fence. "Get to work on his training, then. Show me a profit so I understand why I still keep this place up and running."

He walked away without even saying goodbye. A chill

traveled down my spine. What did he mean?

Joe stretched a hand toward Fire with his palm up. The offer of friendship.

"Sorry about the ruckus today, little pony. The guys were trying to bring you inside. It's going to get bitter cold tonight. Don't you want a nice warm stall to sleep in?"

Fire laid his ears flat and curled his lip.

"Okay, okay," Joe said. "I don't blame you. I'll go. But soon, pony, you and me, we're gonna have to get along."

He picked up a halter off the ground, hung it on the fence, and started toward the barn. I crossed out of the shadows, taking two quick steps toward the paddock, but I'd moved too soon. Joe spun back around. His eyes landed on me.

He knew I was there.

He would tell Mom.

Or Miss May.

If they found out I hadn't told them I wasn't going to the library every day, I'd be in trouble. Maybe Miss May would try to kick Mom and me out.

I'd never see Fire again.

The thought of losing Fire paralyzed me for the few seconds Joe and I stared at each other. But instead of chasing me off, he raised one hand, tipped his head, and walked steadily up the dirt road to the barn. He was gone.

Swirling leaves, the wooden fence, and a blue sky all melded together in front of me. Joe knew I was there with Fire and didn't care. He'd made the other girls leave, but he let me stay. I didn't know what that meant, but air filled my lungs again, and my heart beat steadily. I didn't move until I heard his voice booming from the ring where he was teaching the Thursday afternoon lesson.

"Fire!"

The pony whirled around and snorted, nostrils flared, his neck arched, and his yellow forelock falling over his eyes.

"It's me, Lizzie."

I searched his face for some sign that he recognized me from yesterday. Some sign that he remembered, accepted, and trusted me. He studied me warily, every muscle tense, his ears flicking back and forth. Maybe it was too soon. Maybe I was expecting too much and he needed more time. He shook his head and slowly his body softened. He lifted one hoof from the ground and took a step, stopped, and watched me. I crossed the open area between the woods and fence, eased my hand through the rails, and opened my fingers. One tiny, wrinkled carrot lay in the center of my palm.

Red veins, as thin as sewing thread, spread inside his flared nostrils. His dark eyes shifted between my face and the sad carrot. He was deciding whether to trust me. Something as fragile as trust couldn't be forced. I had to wait.

I would have waited a lifetime.

He took one more step and stopped.

I waited.

Another step.

Then another.

My arm started to ache. I braced it against the fence.

Finally, Fire stretched his neck out, lifted the carrot from my palm, and chewed with his eyes half closed. I didn't move my arm for fear of startling him away. When he finished, he didn't bolt; he didn't lay his ears back or tense up. He lowered his head and sighed. Slowly, I laid trembling fingers against the side of his face. It was warm and familiar. It was like I'd held my hand against that very cheek a thousand times before. He had accepted me. He trusted me.

Somehow, some way, I had to come up with a plan to earn the money to buy him before someone else did. I had to make this pony mine.

"Lizzie?"

I opened my eyes. The room was black. Mom's voice came from her bed below me. My face was wet. I'd been crying in my sleep.

"Hi."

"You were sound asleep when I got home, so I didn't wake you for dinner. Are you hungry?"

I thought of Fire and the way his muzzle tickled my skin when he took the carrot. I touched my palm in the dark, as if doing so could make me feel it again.

"No, I'm not hungry."

"Are you okay?"

"Yeah, why?"

"Miss May said you still go to the library every day. I was

just wondering if you'd made any friends at school."

"I like the library."

Not a lie.

"I do, too. I just want you to be happy. Making friends will be a good thing."

"Okay."

I heard her sigh. "One more thing."

"Yeah?"

"Your dad wrote you another letter."

"Okay."

"Do you want to see it? This is the third one."

"No. He discarded us, so I discard his letters."

All of a sudden, I thought of Joe and Mike talking about the thousand dollars to buy Fire and I bolted upright.

"Wait, Mom. Do you think he'd send money? I mean, it wouldn't make me forgive him, but would he do that?"

"I have no idea. Do you want me to open it and check?"

If there was money, right that second I could start saving to buy Fire.

"Yes, please."

I heard her tear the envelope open, then shuffle through papers.

"No money. I'm sorry."

I flattened myself back against the pillow. "It's not your fault. I should have known."

"Do you want me to read what he wrote?"

"No, thank you."

"Okay. I love you, Lizzie. With all the parts of my heart and soul, I love you."

"I love you, too, Mom. I'm going back to sleep now."

"We're going to get our own place someday. As soon as we get back on our feet, okay? I promise."

"Okay."

And I'm going to find a way to earn money to buy Fire. I promise.

NINE

Friday dawned with drizzling rain soaking the earth. Bryce was absent from school, so for the first time, I used the purple plastic card to buy my lunch. I chose a veggie, fruit, and cheese tray, ate the cheese, then stuffed the carrots, celery, and apple slices into my backpack. Fire would love them. Rain or no rain, nothing would stop me from seeing him. After school, I pulled on my raincoat, jumped a puddle in the small stretch of backyard, and jogged through cold drizzle toward the farm, amazed by the changing look of the path I'd grown to love. The path that took me to my happy place. And now, to Fire.

For the past week, I'd been working on a poem about how everything in the woods behind Birchwood was adapting to the richest part of autumn—the way the air smelled musky instead of summer fresh, the sound drops of rain made when they dripped from naked limbs, the reshaping of the trees, and the whole feel of going from a summer that was vibrant and alive to a fall that was colorless, nearing sleep. I had shown the poem to Ms. Fitzgerald in English earlier in the day.

"This is lovely. Keep working, Lizzie," she'd said. "When you've polished it up, with your permission I'd like to submit it to the high school newspaper. If they accept it, your poem automatically goes into a literary competition. You could win twenty-five dollars."

My ears had perked up when she'd said twenty-five dollars. That amount wasn't even three percent of what it would take to buy Fire. But it was twenty-five dollars closer than I was right then.

"What are the rules?"

"You just need to have it done by Thanksgiving," Ms. Fitzgerald had said. "Can you do that?"

Four weeks. I had four weeks to get it right.

"When would I get the money?"

Ms. Fitzgerald had looked like she wanted to hug me. "I love your spunk, Lizzie. The winner is announced around Valentine's Day."

She'd said I had spunk. I'd never thought of myself as spunky before, but the way she meant it, I liked it. Spunky people made things happen. A spunky person would find a way to earn money to buy Fire. I just had to figure out how.

The afternoon air was fresh and damp, and I ran toward Birchwood feeling energized. On a day like this, no one else would trek down the lane to stand in the cold and wet to see Fire. It would be just him and me. Before I got to the chestnut tree, I could see Fire standing by the tiny shed. Rain drizzled down his face, flattening his forelock. His eyes scanned the woods, and his ears pricked forward, then back, then forward again. He was looking for something. My heartbeat quickened. He was looking for me.

I skirted around the chestnut and was headed toward the grassy strip behind his paddock when my foot snapped a stick in two. It popped like a soggy firecracker, and a body shot up from under a dense veil of brush. Two arms thrashed around near my face.

"Ah!"

I screamed and jumped away, fell to my knees, and rolled onto my back.

Bryce stood beside me with his feet spread apart and his hands out at odd angles like he was ready to karate-chop me to pieces. We stared at each other for two beats, then both cried out, "It's you!" at the same time.

"What are you doing here?" he said. "You scared the flipping eye out of me!"

"What are *you* doing here? I mean, I've never seen you— I was coming to see him."

I pointed to Fire, who was watching us in the dwindling rain. Bryce reached out a hand to help me up.

"Holy smokes, my heart is racing," he said.

I flicked mud from my jeans. "Um, yeah, what do you think mine is doing? And why are you here, anyway?"

"You mean here under the bushes or at Birchwood?"

"Both, I guess."

He let out a breath and shifted his eyes quickly toward the barn. "I'm at Birchwood because my horse came from Wyoming today. That's why I got to stay home from school. But I'm hiding because I don't want to take the stupid equitation lesson my dad signed me up for."

"Wait, what? You have your own horse?"

He jammed his thumbs into his belt. "Yeah, his name is Tucker."

"You keep him here, at Birchwood?"

"As of today, yeah."

"How long have you had him?"

"Four years."

"Oh, wow. How is it I didn't know that? I love horses."

"I figured, since you draw them all the time."

He noticed.

"Why didn't you say something?"

He shrugged. "I dunno. Do you ride here?"

I looked away and changed the subject. “I didn’t know people in Wyoming ride English.”

“People in Wyoming ride everything, but yeah, mostly western. My dad made me do all that stuff. It was hard to find an English trainer who would come as far out as where I lived.”

“You don’t seem like an English equitation kind of rider,” I said.

“I’m not. I’m learning dressage.”

Dressage was like ballet on horseback. It didn’t fit the image of a Wyoming kid who wore cowboy boots and a giant belt buckle.

“You like dressage?”

His body stiffened. “What about it?”

“Nothing,” I said quickly. “I think that’s great.”

He pushed a swath of hair away from his face and clenched his jaw like he didn’t believe me.

“Really,” I said. “I used to watch YouTube videos of Steffen Peters all the time. It just surprised me you like it, that’s all.”

“Sorry. I didn’t mean to get all bucked up,” he said. “My dad promised if I moved to Connecticut with him, I’d get lessons. But once Tucker was on his way, Dad said I have to learn hunter equitation, too, and be on the stupid show team, which I have zero use for whatsoever. My dad thinks dressage is for sissies.”

"He must not know the history of it, like the military part," I said. "It's not for sissies. It was used to train horses for battle, like in something-BC."

Bryce watched my face for a second, then nodded. "He knows all that. He doesn't care. Anyway, wanna see him? My horse, I mean, not my dad. I'll spare you that."

I looked up the hill at the back of the red barn. I'd never dared go any closer than the stone wall. "You mean go inside?"

"Yeah."

"Am I allowed?"

"Why wouldn't you be?"

"I don't know. I thought you had to belong or something."

"Huh," he said. "I never thought of it that way."

Of course he didn't, because he had a dad, and he owned his own horse. He already belonged. Seconds passed. The rain dribbled to a stop. Long streams of sunlight pushed through the clouds moving swiftly over the barn at the top of the hill. Bryce turned toward the muddy road and waved to me over his shoulder.

"Come on," he said.

I followed close behind, trying to control the butterflies whizzing around inside my belly. When we got to the top of the hill, a door on the side of the barn swung open. Joe stepped out, then Kennedy. Joe recognized me right away.

"Well look-y here," he said. "And who is this?"

His eyes crinkled at the corners when he smiled, but

Kennedy scrutinized me, her knuckles jammed into her hips.

"Joe, this is my friend from school," Bryce said. "Lizzie. She came to meet Tucker."

Joe stuck his hand out and winked. "Nice to meet you, Lizzie-from-school. This is Kennedy, former working student, now college student and my number-one instructor extraordinaire."

Kennedy rolled her eyes and shook my hand quickly. "Hey."

"Come on," Bryce said. "Tuck's down here. See you guys later."

Bryce strode ahead of me, eager to get to Tucker's stall, but there was so much to see, and hear, and smell, inside that barn, I lagged behind. The air was both sweet and sour, a mixture of hay and leather and damp horses. The wide aisle had a concrete floor with big stalls flanking it. I recognized a lot of the horses I knew from the fields. A tall bay mare I'd called Princess hung her head over the bottom half of her door, her eyes almost shut and soft putters coming from her lips. A sign said her real name was Tiger Lily.

The smallest pony, the little chestnut with one blue and one brown eye, could barely get her nose over the top of her half-door. I'd called her Sparkle all summer, but her sign said, "Bluebell." Underneath, in bold letters, were clear instructions: "NO GRAIN!" All the way along the aisle, I recognized horses and ponies I'd considered my only friends during the summer.

A dark horse stuck his head out of the last stall on the left and whinnied. A white blaze shaped like a lightning bolt ran from under his forelock to his muzzle. The horse stretched his neck toward us, his ears pricked forward and his nostrils quivering. Bryce quickened his stride.

"That's him!"

He took Tucker's face and kissed his soft muzzle, then scratched behind each ear. "Hey, boy, you doing okay?"

It was hard not to be envious, but I understood exactly how attached Bryce was to his horse. Fire had been at Birchwood only a few days, but I already felt that same kind of bond growing between us.

"He's so pretty," I said. "He's black."

"Technically, he's a dark bay," Bryce said. "See, this is how you tell."

He pointed to faint brown hairs around Tucker's eyes and nose. Then he took a crunchy nugget from his pocket and held it just out of reach.

"Say yes!"

Tucker flung his head up and down.

"Say no!"

He swayed left to right.

"Are you impatient?"

Tucker pawed the ground, then flicked his ears forward and snatched the treat away. I'd never seen Bryce smile like he did right then, as if nothing could possibly be wrong in the world because his horse was here.

"That's really cool," I said.

It was so cool, I had to force myself to keep from sighing.

Bryce brought Tucker out of the stall and swept a soft bristled brush across his black coat, flicking his wrist at the end of each stroke.

"I'll get his hooves picked," he said. "Then we'll walk him outside. Let him stretch his legs some more. He needs it after the long trip."

My stomach squeezed. This was Friday. Jasmine and her crew didn't usually ride on Fridays, but I felt skittish, like being inside the barn wasn't safe. Like I needed to run.

"Actually, I'd better start home soon."

Bryce ran a comb through streams of luxurious black tail hair. Each wave fell like silk against Tucker's hind legs.

"Where do you live? My dad can drive you later if you want."

"It's okay. I live just through there." I pointed in the wrong direction.

Bryce shrugged. "No prob. Next time."

Next time. Please let there be a next time.

"Yeah. And thanks for letting me see Tucker. He's really beautiful." I swung around to leave and body-slammed into Kennedy. "Oh! I'm sorry. I didn't know you were there!"

Bryce pointed the comb at me and laughed. "Two human collisions in one day. You're on a roll."

Kennedy stared blankly, then held out a stack of papers clipped together at the top. "Joe said to give these to you."

"To me? Why?"

She held them up so I could see the heading on the top page. *Birchwood Stables Working Student Program.*

"What are they for?"

"Give them to your parent or guardian," she said with a touch of irritation. "It's about becoming a working student."

"I don't know what that means."

"It's for kids who want to work in exchange for riding lessons instead of paying. Like what I did. All the info is in there." She tapped the top page, then lowered her voice so Bryce couldn't hear. "You're not the first kid to come to us through those woods. It's an opportunity."

Joe must have told her he'd seen me that day. Of course he'd know the path led to Good Hope.

"Anyway," Kennedy said, "there it is. Take them home; bring them back when you can."

She turned to leave and called over her shoulder, "And, Bryce, you know the deal with your dad. I can't teach you dressage if you don't take show team lessons. Don't skip again."

Bryce lifted one of Tucker's back hooves onto his knee and started digging it out with a hoof pick. "K, no prob."

Kennedy strode away. She'd been a working student here. Now she was an instructor. *Instructor extraordinaire.*

I gripped the papers she'd put in my hands and watched her disappear into Tiger Lily's stall with a saddle draped over one arm.

"Come on, Lil," she said, her voice almost musical. "Time for the lessons."

That could be me, I thought. *Someday I could be her.*

TEN

Saturdays were Community Days at Good Hope, which meant we were assigned weekly chores that took up the whole morning. In the haze of my first few months, I hadn't really cared because there wasn't anything else to do. But the day after Kennedy gave me the working student papers, I was antsy, looking for just the right moment to bring them up to Mom. Sharing the papers meant confessing I'd lied about where I'd been going all that time, but Fire was worth the risk.

Mom double-checked the chore sheet when we went for breakfast. "Yup! Still lawn-and-leaf duty!" She sat down with her cup of oatmeal and a big smile on her face. "I've been waiting all fall for that chore."

The rain from the day before had stripped most of the leaves from the trees, which meant there'd be plenty to bag up. And we'd get to do it without Miss May hovering. She'd be inside, supervising all the others while they worked their own chores. Mom and I would have privacy.

After breakfast, Mom buttoned up a red flannel shirt she'd bought at the thrift store and smiled in the mirror. She'd been talking about Saturday all week, hoping it didn't rain, hoping nothing happened that took leaf-raking from her. She always loved fall the best, and lucky for us, Saturday had dawned clear and crisp, greeting us with the dazzling autumn sky she had dreamed about all summer. Miss May gave us two rakes and five giant lawn-and-leaf bags, then sent us outside.

"The acorns!" she called after us. "Be sure you pick up every single acorn or they'll kill the grass!"

Mom and I held in our giggles until we were safely out of range of her hearing.

"She always goes on about the acorns killing the grass," I said, "but how can she think it's the acorns when it's the trees?"

The two old oaks flanked either side of the yard. In the summer, leafy limbs canopied from north to south, east to west, blocking out any possible rays of sun. Acorns dropped in masses onto the ground, but by the time they fell, any grass that had hoped to survive had already withered and died.

"We have to pick them up anyway," Mom said. "Because she said to, and that's what we do for now, okay?"

I stacked the nuts into a pile by the steps, then, to make a rusty moat, scooped red chips from the crumbling bricks around the base of the house. "Why does Miss May complain about these chips clogging up the drains but never has anyone come fix the brick?"

"I'm not sure I know the answer to that, but it isn't my problem, either."

Mom put onto a tree stump an old-timey boom box she'd also gotten at the thrift store, then she cranked up really old music—like Frank Sinatra old—and started swirling around the yard with her rake.

"Come on, Lizzie, dance!" she called. "Don't be shy!"

She pulled her hair from the ponytail holder and danced across the dirt, mouthing the words to the song. In the middle of a twirly circle, she leaned back and let her hair swing out behind her. Frank Sinatra crooned something about the way she looked tonight, and she spun faster and faster and faster until finally, at the end of the song, she let go of the rake. It sailed through the air, and Mom collapsed on the ground in a pile, giggling. I stood over her, feeling like a stranger to the silliness that used to be part of who she was, of who we were before Dad stole all those people's money and everything changed. Before he betrayed us, and we had to hide his shameful secret.

Mom raised herself on her elbows. “It may seem silly to dance with a rake, but honest to god, it feels so good just to dance again.”

She got up and brushed crumpled leaves and dirt from her clothes, then took my chin between her fingers. Her face shined like a long dormant light had been switched back on inside her, and she smelled like baby shampoo and earth and mint.

“We can’t ever forget, Lizzie,” she said, her cool blue eyes studying mine. “We must always remember how it feels to be normal so we’ll recognize it when we get there again.”

I let the whole weekend pass without saying anything about Birchwood. Being outdoors made Mom so happy, I was afraid my confession would ruin her mood. On Saturday night, she and Linda finally went to that movie they’d been talking about. I worried all evening that Linda would say something about my absence at the library during the week, but Mom came home humming a tune, kissed me, and went right to bed.

On Monday, Bryce stopped me in the hallway between third and fourth periods.

“Hey!” he said. “I have a dentist appointment so I’m leaving, but I’ll see you at the barn later.”

He gave me a thumbs-up before being swallowed by a crowd of kids who were deliberately still strangers to both of us. But that didn't matter because I was going back to Birchwood after school. I'd been invited inside the barn again. I ducked my head to hide my smile and walked within a hair's distance of Rikki and Sabrina, who were huddled together by their lockers. They'd heard Bryce.

"What barn?" Rikki asked.

I looked away like I didn't hear her and sped past.

If it weren't for the nagging memory of Jasmine staring at me through the trees that day when I was straddling the stone wall, I wouldn't have cared as much. If I had just started going to Birchwood as Bryce's friend, it would be different. But she had seen me. Even though she'd never said anything since school started, any question she might ask could lead to more of them about my family. I had to keep my guard up and not give anyone the ammunition MaryBeth had when she'd humiliated and shunned me. Not until the whole Dad thing was over.

It wasn't like I'd been doing anything wrong when Jasmine saw me. There weren't any "No Trespassing" signs in those woods. But it was weird. If I were one of those girls and saw some stranger straddling a stone wall and spying on the riding lessons, I'd want to know why, too.

After school, it took less than two minutes for me to sign in and out in Miss May's book and throw my backpack through the door to our room. I raced down the path toward Birchwood, excited to see both Fire and Bryce. Seeing them would give me courage to talk to Mom after dinner, and after that—after she agreed for me to be a working student—I could be inside Birchwood every single day and it wouldn't matter who saw me there. I would belong.

Veering right at the fork, I picked up my pace, wove through the twisty trail, and came up behind the chestnut, out of breath, and slammed to a halt. The dust in Fire's paddock lay quiet. The halter and lead rope that usually hung from his fence were gone. The gate was tied open. A few pieces of hay tumbled across the ground, rising when the wind picked them up and carried them away. In the distance, nearing the top of the hill, Fire struggled against Robert and Luis, the two men who worked in the barn. Luis was leaning back against a lead rope attached to Fire's halter, and Robert was pushing his hindquarters.

Fire reared and screamed so loud the sound carried across the hills and landed in my ears like an alarm. Robert and Luis yelled and closed in, surrounding him like a shackled prisoner. The last I saw was Robert dodging away, his knees narrowly escaping a strike from Fire's back hooves. Then the three of them disappeared inside the barn.

I dug my fingernails into the bark of the chestnut tree, listening to the sound of silence as the chill of the autumn wind wrapped ugly arms around me. Fire was gone, and I was right back in that kitchen the day Dad left, watching Mom weep, with no idea how everything I'd known in my life had just been stolen from me. I sank to my knees, watching the barn, hoping to see Fire bolt from inside and gallop up the road to me, but all remained quiet.

I don't know how long I'd been kneeling in the dirt before I saw Bryce, already halfway up the lane, waving his arms to get my attention. "Lizzie!"

I jumped up and wiped my face in the crook of my elbow. Bryce stopped where he was and raised both hands in question.

"Are you coming?"

"Are you sure it's okay?"

"It's okay if you don't make me late for my lesson," he called. "Hurry!"

I ran down the lane and caught up with him. We walked quickly up the hill, into the barn, and down to Tucker's stall.

"They put that pony you like in there." He pointed directly across the aisle from Tucker. "Don't go in there; he's pretty wild. You should have seen them trying to get him in the barn."

"I did," I said. "It was awful."

"Hope you don't like him too much," Bryce said. "Not sure how long they'll keep a pony that nasty around, no matter how fancy he is. Luis has teeth marks on his arm."

When Bryce kneeled down to wrap Tucker's legs, I darted across and stuck my head over the stall door. Fire was braced against the far wall, his ears flattened, and one back hoof cocked in warning. A fresh flake of hay lay untouched in front of him.

"Fire," I whispered. "It's me. I'm here."

He unflattened his ears and flicked them back and forth, but he didn't come. I held out half an apple.

"It's okay, buddy. I saw what happened. You're okay."

I talked softly, mumbling things over and over until finally he turned his head and looked at me.

"You have to come here to get the apple," I said quietly. "I can't go in there."

"That's exactly right!" Kennedy's voice boomed sharply behind me.

I startled, and Fire flung himself against the wall again.

"No one goes in with him at all. He's loco," she said, rolling her index finger in a circle around her ear.

"Oh, he isn't—" Behind her, Bryce held his finger up to his lips and shook his head at me.

"Hey, Kennedy, Lizzie's coming to watch the lesson. That okay?"

Kennedy looked me up and down, shrugged, and stalked away. "Your money. I'll meet you in the ring."

"You do want to watch, right?" Bryce asked. "I mean, you don't have to. I just thought since you like dressage and all—"

I tossed the apple inside Fire's stall.

"I definitely want to watch," I said.

He smiled and nodded, then handed me his helmet to carry as I followed him to a small sandy ring on the other side of the barn.

"This ring is used only for private lessons," Bryce said to me, tightening Tucker's girth. "I'm just saying, so if you ever come and can't find me, I might be in here. You can come anytime, you know."

Kennedy moved a black rubber step stool from behind a wall. "Here, sit on the mounting block," she said, dropping it in the center of the ring. "Advanced riders like Bryce aren't allowed to use it to mount, only beginners."

I sat obediently while Bryce focused everything on warming up Tucker at a walk. It was like, once he was on his horse's back, they became one, like no one else was there, no one else needed to be there. It was exactly the way I imagined it would be when I rode Fire someday. Because after watching Bryce with Tucker, I knew, without any uncertainty, I would ride Fire, and he would be mine.

Kennedy sipped coffee from a green cup and watched the pair move around the ring. There was another full cup of coffee in a box on the block next to me, with a peach-and-gold rose on the side and *O'Toole's Pub* written underneath.

Kennedy downed her first cup and traded for the full one. "Okay, get him moving. Trot some serpentines, do some figure eights, make him bend and stretch. We've got a lot of work to do today."

I could hear people out in the barn getting their horses and ponies ready for lessons. Hooves clomped up and down the concrete aisle, stall doors rolled open and closed, kids called for help saddling ponies, and Joe's voice was in the midst of it all. "Hustle, hustle, hustle, guys. You're missing valuable lesson time!"

Bryce didn't seem to hear a thing except the words from Kennedy's mouth. His face was set like a stone for most of the lesson. But when Tucker moved in a particular way, even though I couldn't tell for sure what he was doing differently, Bryce beamed and glanced over quickly to see if I'd noticed. After about forty minutes of work, both horse and rider were drenched in sweat.

"Good job. Get him cooled out," Kennedy said. "You're coming along. Keep practicing."

She picked up her coffee trash and walked out with barely a nod to me.

Bryce dismounted, loosened the girth, and walked Tucker in circles to cool him off, a small, satisfied smile curving his mouth up at the corners.

"You guys looked great," I said.

He took off his helmet and ran his fingers through damp hair. "Thanks. Kennedy makes us work, but that's exactly what I wanted."

"Did she not want me here?" I asked.

"What do you mean?"

"She was just—I don't know—snippy, like she was irritated I was watching or something."

"Nah. She's just weird that way. Distant. Doesn't talk much until you know her. She'll be friendlier next time."

Next time. My belly tickled.

"Hey," Bryce said. "The indoor polo season starts Friday night. Wanna go hot-walk the ponies with me? The riders pay pretty well, plus it's fun. We could pick you up at your house and bring you home afterward."

I'd never even seen a polo match on YouTube and had only a vague idea what hot-walking ponies meant, but I was all ready to say yes until he said the part about picking me up and taking me home.

"Oh, Friday, um, I can't—I have something to do with my mom that night. But thanks anyway. And thanks for letting me come watch your lesson. It was cool."

I left soon after, running straight between the fields toward the path in the woods, thinking about what Bryce had said about polo. If I could figure out how to get there and back without him picking me up at Good Hope, it was a way to earn money for Fire. Once again, the bitterness toward Dad and all he'd done to complicate our lives rose in my throat. I was almost to the split in the trail when a single orange leaf fluttered to the ground in front of me. It was probably one of the last in all of Connecticut with any hint of color. I stopped to pick it up, rubbed my fingers up and down the lobes, then put it to my nose and inhaled the familiar smell of autumn woods.

Every fall before Dad got weird, he and I used to gather sprays of orange and red leaves for our scrapbook. Mom would iron each spray between pieces of wax paper as carefully as she ironed Dad's shirts, pressing the tips of the leaves all the way to the edges so they wouldn't curl and dry out. Then we'd glue them onto the ivory pages of the scrapbook to preserve them forever.

Now, I carried this leaf carefully back to Good Hope and tucked it between the pages of the working student papers. The scrapbook, the one with all the leaves from our old life, was packed inside a box somewhere, and *forever* would never mean the same again.

ELEVEN

When Mom got home, I was waiting on the bed with the Birchwood papers stashed behind me. I'd rehearsed in my head a hundred times what I was going to say. I was ready. But then she burst into the room, her eyes all bright and shiny, waving two one-hundred-dollar bills in the air.

"Guess what? I got a bonus today for getting the office through a big project!"

She hung her jacket on the door where we'd Velcroed a coat hook. The rule list had specified no nails, no picture-hanger things, and no hooks bolted into the walls. So, we'd gotten the Velcro kind and tested it to see how many jackets we could hang before it fell off. One.

"And I earned a half day off, so as soon as you're home from school tomorrow, we're going clothes shopping!"

She stood in front of me with this big goofy smile like she expected me to jump off the bed and dance around the room.

I didn't want to go shopping.

I wanted to tell her about Birchwood. And if we were going to spend money on anything, once I became a working student, I would need boots and a helmet.

"I don't need clothes," I said.

"You do need clothes, and we need a Mom-and-Lizzie adventure. We'll take the bus to Hartford."

"We can just get some stuff at the thrift store. Remember they had jeans for five dollars?"

And riding clothes.

"You turned your nose up at them."

"Well, I changed my mind. We should be saving money, in case we need something more important than regular old clothes."

She put the back of her hand to my forehead. "You feeling okay?"

"Yeah, I'm fine."

"The arms of your jacket don't even come to your wrists. This is a chance to get a new coat that will last. Are you sure you're feeling okay?"

I leaned my back against the wall so the Birchwood

papers were completely hidden, and made up an excuse for my melancholy. "I'm just tired of walking into the bathroom and finding the toilet full of throw-up."

"Are Angela's kids sick?"

"They're always sick. They throw up more than any kids I've ever known. Shouldn't they go to the doctor or something?"

"Doctors are expensive, Lizzie," she said sharply. "Maybe Angela doesn't have health insurance. Kids throw up. Even I didn't run off to the doctor every single time you did."

"But shouldn't Angela at least flush the toilet?"

Mom folded her work blazer over the back of the chair and sighed. "No judging, young lady. She is a single mom with no support. It wouldn't hurt you to offer to help her from time to time."

"Only if there's something I can do that doesn't involve stinky diapers," I grumbled to myself.

Regardless of my objections, we took the bus to Hartford the next afternoon. I'd never been to Hartford, and I'd never stepped foot inside a Walmart. In our Life Before, we shopped at the boutiques in our town. Sometimes we took the train into New York City, had lunch with Dad, and went shopping at the big fancy stores.

But that was then.

The Walmart aisles were jam-packed with people piling Halloween decorations, candy, and costumes into their carts.

We wandered around for fifteen minutes with our arms full of jackets and jeans before finding a dressing room. The first one still had a pile of clothes on the bench. We moved on until we found one that was empty.

"These prices are good, Lizzie," Mom said. "Get whatever you want."

It wasn't until I tried on a coat that actually fit that I realized Mom had been right about the old one. The new one was puffy and pink, almost the same color as the Birchwood jackets, with secret pockets inside just the right size for horse treats. We headed off for the bus stop, loaded down with plastic bags.

"For someone who didn't want to go shopping, you didn't do so bad," Mom said when we settled into our seats.

In addition to two turtlenecks, a lavender hoodie, two sweaters, underwear, socks, sneakers, and two pairs of jeans, she'd let me get a stack of six spiral notebooks in assorted colors and a box of nice, sharp number two pencils. Not too shabby, indeed.

I pressed my forehead against the window and let my breath make a little circle of steam on the glass. The bus lurched forward. I drew a picture of Fire in the steam, then wiped it away with my arm and watched the busy people rushing along the sidewalk as the evening light faded. It wasn't fully dark yet, but all the streetlamps flicked on. We stopped again to pick up more passengers, then chugged forward in traffic at the same pace as everyone on the sidewalk.

Mothers and kids, businesspeople, construction workers, couples, and Dad.

I jumped up and screamed. "Mom, it's Dad! Look!"

Her whole face froze. He was so close, if it weren't for the glass between us and the traffic noise, he would have heard me. He strode purposefully beside the bus, in and out of the light, unaware that we were right there. I reached out to bang on the window, but Mom grabbed my arm and pushed me down into the seat, her fingers clasped tightly around my hands.

"Stop," she said harshly. "Leave it alone."

Her voice was cold, but her eyes were on fire. Her face flushed with something that frightened me. The brakes squealed as the bus came to another stop. Dad stopped, too, and draped his arm over the shoulders of a blond lady wearing high heels and glittery earrings. A teenage girl in a dressy coat and scarf stood between them. Her eyes were glued to Dad's face. She threw her head back and laughed at whatever he was saying. The lady laughed, too, and the three of them turned together like water ballerinas and walked away.

"Dad?" It was barely more than a whisper.

My whole body slumped. Every molecule of air was sucked from my lungs. I couldn't breathe. The bus jerked forward, and my back slammed against the seat, releasing the hold on my chest. I gasped for air and watched out the window as individual strangers blended into one mass of people. Dad had disappeared. He was one of them now, a stranger. He didn't even know we'd been there.

Mom didn't say anything for the longest time. We sat on the bus, our shopping bags in our laps, staring straight ahead, expressionless, as the lights of the city fell behind us and we traveled through the dark for the thirty minutes it took to get back to our new town. Finally, she took my hand and squeezed three times.

"I'm so sorry, Lizzie."

I laid my head on her shoulder and closed my eyes.

It was past eleven o'clock, but Mom's tiny reading light shined a V on the wall from below. We hadn't spoken much since we got home. Neither of us could sleep. I took the Birchwood working student papers out of the notebook and held them up against the wall so the light illuminated the words.

"Mom?"

"Yes?"

"Did you know about the girl?"

I could hear her close her book. "No. I'm so sorry."

"Is that where he lives?"

"I don't know. But next time we need something, we won't go to Hartford."

She got up and went down the hall to the bathroom. The orange leaf fell from between the pages of the Birchwood papers. I examined it in the light, then dug my fingernail into the brilliant orange blade, crushed it into a million bits, and threw it against the wall. The pieces scattered like orange confetti. Mom came back, silently got into her bed, and switched off the reading lamp.

"Mom?"

"Yes?"

"I have something to tell you."

Pause. "That sounds ominous."

"There's a horse farm on the other side of the woods."

Silence.

"I know we can't pay for anything. I'm not asking that."

"Is it near the library?"

"Sort of. It's down that other path, the one that goes right at the fork."

"Okay."

"There's a pony there. He's new. I named him Fire."

"Ooo-kaaay."

Deep breath.

"There's a boy at school who keeps his horse there. He just moved from Wyoming. He let me come into the barn to meet him—Tucker, that's his horse's name—and I met the guy who runs the stable. His name is Joe."

Her covers rustled and she flipped the reading light back on.

"When did all this take place?"

"The whole thing or just the Joe part?"

"I guess the whole thing."

Deeper breath.

"I've been going in the afternoons and watching the lessons. I didn't want to tell you because I was afraid you'd say I couldn't go."

"What about the library?"

"I still go sometimes but mostly on Saturdays."

"Did you think I'd tell you not to go because you weren't allowed there?"

"I didn't want you to think I was going to ask you to pay for anything. And also, well, kind of because it was the only place that was all mine."

Mom pushed her covers off. The bunk jiggled when she sat up. "And what made you decide to tell me now?"

I climbed down and curled up next to her with my head on her shoulder, and I told her the whole thing. Everything. Including how I never felt I belonged anywhere anymore and about the poems I wrote. I told her how afraid Fire was when he came but that he trusted me, only me. I told her how sad I was when I heard that Fire would be for sale someday because that meant he could lose his home all over again.

I let those words settle for a second, to let them sink in. For her and for me. Then I told her about Bryce and how he took me into the barn like it was no big deal and how I was both jealous and happy about the way Tucker loved him. And finally, after I had told her everything else, after I told her about Kennedy giving me the papers for the working student program and how she'd said I wasn't the first kid to come to them through the woods, I told Mom about going there the day before and finding Fire gone and how it made me feel the same way I felt on the day Dad left and I found her crying in the kitchen.

As soon as I told her that part, she asked to see the papers. And that was that.

TWELVE

Mom called Joe from her office the next day and made arrangements for us to meet at Birchwood on Sunday morning. She asked me not to go back again until everything was settled and she'd seen it for herself. That meant I had to wait four whole days to see Fire again.

"What if Bryce invites me?"

"Just let it float, Lizzie. Four days won't kill you. Put your attention on things that need it right now."

So, I opened one of the new notebooks and started writing.

TO BUY FIRE

$1,000

– 25 (if I win the poetry contest)

$975 to buy Fire

On Friday night, I woke up well after midnight and tiptoed down the hall to the bathroom. Angela hadn't emptied the trash can again—a habit she apologized for every day. The cramped room was thick with odor. I tied up the bag, sprayed linen-scented Lysol everywhere, and slipped out the back door, tossing the bag into the Dumpster on top of the orange-and-black crepe paper streamers that Miss May had already discarded from Halloween.

Above me, a three-quarter moon hovered in a navy sky. Misty yellow light lingered in the woods, illuminating the start of the path like it was an invitation. Tiny crystals of frost shimmered on swaying branches, and before I knew what I was doing, I was halfway to the chestnut tree, running along the path in only my slippers, flannel pajamas, and bathrobe. I wasn't afraid of being alone in the night, not in these woods. From the edge of Fire's old paddock, the strange light almost made the barn look haunted and slightly crooked at the top of that hill. Sprinting through the woods, I scaled the stone wall, darted across the frost-coated ring, and pushed open the big door just enough to squeeze inside. The horses heard me and, thinking it was breakfast time, rattled their buckets and nickered for food. A big chestnut gelding named Samson pawed the floor with hooves the size of dinner plates.

"Shhhh, Samson, be quiet!"

Fire was hidden in the darkest corner. I slipped inside his stall and stood by the door.

"It's me, Fire," I whispered. "I'm here."

I waited for him to come, just like I'd waited those first days when he was in the paddock by the woods. After a few minutes of coaxing, he moved cautiously toward me, close enough so I could bury my face in his neck and inhale the sweet smell of pony and hay and love.

"You're going to be mine someday, Fire," I whispered. "I promise."

By seven o'clock Sunday morning, I was dressed and bouncing around the room, waiting for Mom to wake up. She peeked out from under the covers.

"Lizzie, it's too early for all that energy. Go back to bed. We aren't supposed to be there until ten."

She hid her head under the blanket. I pulled it off and got up close to her face.

"Well, Mom, it's actually snowing. I was thinking it might take us longer to walk through the woods."

I opened the curtains for her to see soft flakes drifting from a gray sky.

"It's barely November," she said. "How can it already be snowing?"

"Look, there's even frost on the windowsill."

She raised up, her face just showing under a mop of messy hair.

"That path is probably too slippery for us to walk on today," she said, trying to hide a grin. "We should postpone."

I plunked down next to her and gave the most pitiful, orphan-like expression I could muster. "Don't you want to see all the places in the woods I love?"

We were out the door at eight thirty. Even though only a couple inches of snow lay on the ground, we bundled up in scarves and mittens and snow boots for the first time that fall. Mom snuck a real ceramic mug full of hot coffee out of the kitchen to sip on the walk over.

"That just means you have to sneak the cup back in, you know," I said.

She held it between mittened hands and smiled at me over the rim. Steam swirled in front of her face. "And what do you know about sneaking in and out, little missy, hmmm?"

She had been fast asleep when I'd gone to see Fire in the middle of the night, I was positive. If she suspected what I'd done, she would have said something. I let the moment linger, waiting to see what she actually knew. Finally, I put my hands together in front of myself and bowed.

"I speak from the voice of experience."

She laughed and reached an arm out to squeeze my shoulder. "I haven't seen you this happy in so long."

"I haven't felt this happy in a long time."

She followed me along the path until I stopped at the

bend, where a red cardinal flitted about in front of us. We watched him dart from one frosted branch to another, and listened to the hush broken only by the gentle sound of snow falling from the trees to the earth. All around us, the woods were sparkly, magical, and silent.

"Sometimes it's like I'm walking through a Robert Frost poem when I come here," I whispered.

Mom tightened her periwinkle-blue scarf around her neck. She'd made the scarf herself, with yarn given to her by a man she knew through work who had taught her how to crochet during lunch breaks. Her eyes were the same color as the yarn, and her skin reminded me again of her favorite peach roses from the garden back home. She was so pretty. I resisted reaching out to touch her face and touched mine instead, wishing I looked more like her than like Dad.

She cupped her hand against my cheek. "What is your favorite poem these days, Lizzie?"

We walked side by side and talked about things we'd forgotten to talk about for a very long time. Important things, like poems, and ice cream, and books. For a little while, it felt like everything was normal again. When we came up behind the chestnut tree, Mom put her hand out to stop me, staring at the magic that was Birchwood Stables on the first snowy morning of the year.

"I had no idea it would be so pretty," she said. "It's breathtaking."

My heart ballooned. I'd been so preoccupied with keeping

my distance from anyone who might find out about Dad, I'd forgotten how good it felt to share things that mattered. Especially with Mom.

"I really wanted you to love it," I said.

She took the last sip of coffee and set the mug down in the middle of the path where we'd see it on our way home.

"How did you find this farm?"

"Remember the day you went to testify?"

Her face clouded over for a second and she nodded.

"I came that day. Then almost every day after you started working."

"What did you do?"

"I sat there," I said, pointing to my spot at the edge of the woods, "and wrote poems, and drew pictures, and watched the horses."

"By yourself?"

I nodded. She stayed silent for a few minutes, her eyes sweeping over the landscape. I pointed to the far side of the barn near the ring.

"Over there is a stone wall where I watched people take lessons."

"Oh, sweetie." She pulled me close and kissed the top of my head. "That must have hurt."

"Sometimes, but I got to learn," I said. "Are you mad that I didn't tell you?"

Her eyes teared up. "I've been so worried you haven't made friends at school, I'm just grateful you had this place."

"Everything is okay, Mom," I said. "Besides, it's just until we're back on our feet, remember?"

She swung our joined hands in front of us. "Come on, do you think Joe will mind if we're an entire hour early?"

Joe didn't mind one bit. His eyes crinkled when he opened the office door and ushered us in.

"I had a feeling we'd be meeting early." He put his hand out to Mom. "I'm Joe, the farm manager. Or at least that's the rumor."

Mom's cheeks flushed. "Nice to meet you," she said. "And thank you for—well, for inviting Lizzie and all of this."

"Of course, I can tell a real horse-girl from miles away. Horse-girls keep me in business, so—"

His voice was cut off by a familiar whinny ringing out from the other end of the barn. Fire. He knew I was there. Joe stepped aside.

"You can see him while your mom and I talk; just don't go into the stall."

Fire whinnied again. I burst out the door and strode down that aisle, past Bluebell and Tiger Lily and all the others, my heart pounding until I reached his stall. He was waiting for me, his head hanging over the half door. I reached up and scratched under his forelock, my heart soaring.

Kennedy came half an hour later with a clipboard in one hand, a coffee in the other, and Mom not far behind. "I can't schedule you for any real working student hours until Thursday," Kennedy said, "because I'm going on a school trip. I need to be here during your first few days of work. But! We'll do your orientation now, then you can study everything and be ready to rock and roll on Thursday."

She turned away and started calling out horse's names over her shoulder, pointing to their nameplates on the stall doors as we passed.

"Note the signs on the stalls, especially when they have to do with grain. Do you know what colic is?"

I nodded.

"Founder?"

I nodded again.

"Good. Then you know how serious too much grain can be."

"Yes."

Kennedy rattled on. Tack room. Wash stall. Cross-ties. Bootjack. Martingales. Hay. Shavings. Grain. Feed room. Tack lockers. Ponies. Horses. Don't give a hot horse cold water to drink. Student list. Lesson schedule. Horse/pony requests. Sign-in and -out sheets. Be on time. Stay through your shift. Answer the phone cheerfully. Wipe sweat and dirt from saddles before putting away. Put fresh saddle pads with clean saddles and throw the dirty pads in the wash-room. Dip bits in water and clean off saliva. Pick out hooves both before and after horses are ridden. Smell the hoof pick for thrush.

"Do you know what thrush is?" she asked, peering at me over the clipboard.

I nodded again.

"Tell me," she said.

"It's a fungal infection in their hooves. It damages the sensitive part on the underside and smells really bad and makes them lame if it isn't treated."

"Good work," she said, making a giant check mark on her list. She handed me a folder of papers. "Read these and study the diagrams at home. Think you've got it?"

I took the folder and nodded. I wasn't about to tell her the whole idea of memorizing everything by Thursday was so overwhelming, my stomach was shaking.

"Good," she said briskly. "I know it's a lot, but Joe or I will always be here if you have questions, and I think you've seen enough over the last few months that most of this should feel familiar."

She walked away, her boot heels scraping the floor. Mom and I followed her to the office, where she nodded brusquely to Joe.

"She's got it," Kennedy said, flipping through some pages of the working student logbook. "Thursday, four o'clock, we start. Sound good?"

I squeezed the folder tight. My whole body felt like it might burst from joy. "Got it."

"Great, see you then. Gotta run. Nice to meet you," she said to Mom before rushing out the door.

Joe watched her leave and laughed. "She's a busy one, but thank god I've got her on my team."

* * *

"I have to wait four more days before I see Fire again," I said wistfully that night.

"Make good use of the time," Mom said.

"What does that mean?"

"People are reaching out to do nice things for you, Lizzie. This is a great opportunity to pay it forward. Do something nice for someone else."

"Like what? And who?"

"You have a brain. Figure it out."

THIRTEEN

At dinner on Monday, Angela dragged the three girls into the dining room with dark circles under her eyes. Her hair hung around her shoulders like red tinsel that had been recycled too many times. All three girls clung to her, whimpering. Mrs. Ivanov smiled sadly from her place at the table.

"Khotel by ya pomoch'," she said.

Leonard brought her plate of lasagna and sat down, cutting his eyes at me. "She says she wishes to help," he said curtly.

I looked at Mom to see if she noticed the way Leonard

always acted like he couldn't stand me, but just then Hope started squealing.

"No, no, no!"

She jerked her arm away from Angela and tried to hit her thigh.

"No! I say no!"

Everyone in the room stopped to watch the struggle going on at our table, but no one did anything to help. I grabbed Charity from the floor and buckled her into the high chair, then sat down and helped Faith climb into my lap. Angela was kneeling beside her chair with both arms wrapped tight around Hope.

"Shhh, sweet baby girl, let's just get dinner, then we'll snuggle up in bed and I'll read you a book, okay?"

She took Hope by the hand and led her, wailing, to the food table.

"What else should I do?" I asked Mom.

"Exactly what you are," she said.

She got up and helped Angela bring plates of food for the girls. I opened a purple jar of baby-food blueberries and spooned some into Charity's mouth, cooing like I'd seen Angela do. Charity smushed the berries around in her mouth and giggled. I separated Faith's lasagna into bite-sized chunks in a Styrofoam bowl and let her pick up the pieces with her fingers. Mom put a plate of lasagna in front of me and another in front of Angela. Mrs. Ivanov saw I had one baby with a blue face and another kid smeared with red, and she passed down a fresh roll of paper towels. All the while, Angela kept trying to coax Hope to eat.

"Please," she pleaded. "The social workers will take you away again if they think I'm not feeding you."

Hope tightened her lips and squeezed her eyes shut. For twenty minutes, the three of us worked together to get Angela's kids fed. Mom refilled our water glasses and wiped faces and hands with a wet cloth. I fed Faith and Charity, then entertained them with Itsy Bitsy Spider and other simple games while Hope flailed her arms and cried. Everyone else in the room ate fast and fled.

"I'm sorry about your dinner," Angela said, wiping a tear from her eye. "I'm sure it's cold by now."

"One cold dinner is nothing," Mom said. "I'm glad we were here to help."

"I'm so tired. Sometimes I feel like giving up."

I looked quickly at Mom. What did Angela mean, *"give up"*?

"We're all here because we need some extra help for a while," Mom said quickly. "Never be afraid to ask."

"Yeah," I echoed. "It was fun."

"Fun?" Angela smiled for the first time that evening. "What are you doing at dinnertime tomorrow?"

Later that night I found a folded piece of paper under the soap dish in the bathroom with my name written on it. Inside was a note from Angela and a five-dollar bill.

I couldn't have survived tonight without your help. Or the other day when you took the dirty diaper trash out. Thank you. Save this for something special.

I knew better than to keep the money. With three little girls, Angela's Back on Her Feet was probably going to take a lot longer than ours. She needed the five dollars more than I did. Still, I hid it between the pages of my notebook. I wasn't ready to give it up, because holding that piece of green paper in my hand made my dream of buying Fire feel the tiniest bit more real.

TO BUY FIRE
$1,000
– 25 (if I win the poetry contest)
$975 to buy Fire
– $5 (Angela)
$970 to buy Fire

The next day I took the path to the left and actually did go to the library. Linda had a line of people at her desk and didn't see me come in. But Leonard did. He caught me moving swiftly through the World History section, where he was running his fingers along the book spines.

"Zdravstvuyte," he said.

I had no idea what that meant, but from the way Leonard glared at me, I was pretty sure I didn't want to know. I ignored him and kept going until I got to the small section of horse and pony books. I bypassed the well-worn paperback series with pictures of perfect ponies and jewels and rainbows on the covers. I'd read *Black Beauty* three times since we'd moved, plus everything they had in the Black Stallion series, and I had devoured anything else that didn't seem like the cover should have a unicorn on it instead of a real horse. But never once had I thought to look for any books on the cost of owning my own pony. Not until Fire.

There was only one: a hardcover called *The Affordable Horse* with a picture of a fat white gelding on the cover. I scanned through the pages quickly, then headed to the line to check it out. Leonard snuck up behind me and leaned over my shoulder, reading the title out loud.

"*The Affordable Horse*," he said. "Why do you need that book?"

I tucked it under my armpit. "It's for a friend," I said.

"You have rich friends you keep secret?"

His words made my spine cramp. I turned sharply away to move from the line. His hand shot out to stop me.

"Wait," he said.

"No, I have to get something else."

I jerked away and rushed up the stairs to the thrift store to hide until he left. From the top of the steps, where the riding apparel was still on display, I could pretend to look at the clothes and watch the desk at the same time. Only three pairs of paddock boots were left. The tall show boots were gone, but above the remaining boots, a navy-blue riding coat hung from a rack.

"Hey, look who's here!"

It was Jasmine, with Jade at her side, coming up the steps.

"Are you buying something?" Jasmine asked.

Ever since she had seen me hiding in the woods pretending the stone wall was a horse, I'd been waiting for the moment when she would tell on me to her friends. I'd been dreading it. I covered *The Affordable Horse* title with my hand.

"No, just checking how much I might get for my old riding clothes."

One hundred percent lie.

"You don't get all the money, you know," Jade said. "You get half and the thrift store gets the other half. That's my old show jacket, there."

She pointed to the blue coat.

"I'm aware," I said. "Excuse me, I have to go."

I squeezed past them and darted down the steps, disappearing among the rows of books. I found an empty bench at the back near the restrooms and buried my face in the pages of my book, waiting now not just for Leonard to leave but Jasmine and Jade, too. I'd read twelve pages before the coast was clear.

"Hey there, young lady, how are you?" Linda asked cheerfully when I got to the checkout.

"Okay," I said. I handed her *The Affordable Horse*. "I'm getting this for a friend in school."

She tapped the cover and smiled. "Oh, I dreamed about owning a horse when I was a kid."

"Yeah, I just saw it and thought, you know, it would be nice to let her read it, since she wants to get a horse."

It felt awful lying to Linda, but I wasn't ready to tell anyone else about my plan to buy Fire. I didn't want anyone telling me it was impossible, and I didn't want anyone telling me I should give whatever money I saved to Mom. Especially if that anyone was me.

By the time my first working student day finally arrived, I was beat from helping Angela with the girls at dinner each night, but I was also richer.

I marked down every bit of money in my book and watched the numbers change. Sometimes, I opened the notebook just to see the numbers lined up in the column, even if I didn't have anything to add.

When I got to Birchwood after school, Kennedy was waiting for me in the office.

"Hey, kiddo, you ready?"

"Yeah."

"What's the first thing you do?"

Suddenly, everything she'd taught me went right out of my head. Tacking? Grooming? Feeding? Watering? What was it?

Kennedy pushed the working student logbook across Joe's desk.

"Oh, right! Sign in," I said.

"Yup, you sign in."

I wrote in my name and in the next column marked the time: 3:53 p.m. My first day. I resisted drawing a giant happy face on the page.

For the next two hours, I shadowed Kennedy and another girl named Meridy, who had been a working student for over a year already.

"She can be your mentor if I'm not around," Kennedy told me. "But she's moving to Hawaii in two weeks, so learn fast, okay?"

At six o'clock Mom surprised me by showing up. She was in the office with Kennedy when I went to sign out.

"So how'd you like it?" Kennedy asked.

"Great!" I said.

"Well, you won't be able to have your first full lesson until you've worked more hours," she said, "but I told your mom to come because I think Joe has made arrangements for you to ride Rusty for a few minutes."

"Today?"

She raised her eyebrows. *Affirmative.*

I dropped the pen. "Right now?"

"Right now," she said. "You have a date waiting for you in the little indoor ring."

My feet didn't want to stay on the ground; they wanted to dance the whole way to the ring. I was going to ride a pony.

Right then.

That very day.

Finally.

Kennedy brought Mom and me through a wooden gate to where Joe was walking the ancient, swayback pony in a circle. Each time one of Rusty's front hooves hit the ground, his knobby knees turned out, and his belly swung to the side. Scrawny tufts of red hair made their way up his neck, ending at a pom-pom of fuzz between his ears. His face was peppered with gray hairs around his eyes and his muzzle.

"Rusty may not look like much," Joe said, "but this pony has carried hundreds, maybe thousands, of kids on his back over the years. He's our best beginner pony. He'll keep you good and safe."

Rusty was a far cry from Fire, but right that second, I didn't care. He smelled like ponies and saddles, and when he reached out his muzzle and looked at me with soft, gentle eyes, my heart got all squishy and I knew I could love him, too.

Kennedy pulled his girth tight. "Do you know how to mount?"

"I—I think so," I stammered. "I mean, I've seen it, and kind of practiced it but not on a real pony."

"Yeah, well, it'll be a little different from practicing on a stone wall," she said playfully. "But let's give it a try. I'll go get you a helmet."

Joe handed me a pair of old, scuffed-up paddock boots that sagged at the ankle. "Try these on. They should work."

Kennedy found a green helmet that fit my head perfectly

and buckled it under my chin. I turned to show Mom.

"You look like an equestrian," she said. "My Lizzie the equestrian."

"Okay, kiddo," Joe said, "let's see what you know."

He handed over Rusty's reins. The three of them watched me stand next to his left shoulder and weave my fingers into the tiny bit of mane at his withers. My left foot slipped easily into the metal stirrup. I pushed off the ground with my right leg, and in one slightly clumsy movement, I was sitting on Rusty's back.

"Nicely done," Kennedy said.

"Welcome to freedom, Lizzie," Joe said. "It's the start of something beautiful."

Joe was right. It was beautiful, and I did feel free in a way that was hard to put into words. But the best part was, I hadn't needed Dad to make it happen after all.

WINTER

FOURTEEN

The third time Fire pulled the Christmas wreath from his stall door, I almost gave up.

"You're so bad," I said, sticking the candy canes and what was left of three hot-glued sugar cubes back onto the cedar-and-pine ring. "Mom and I worked hard on this."

A fuzzy carrot-and-holly ornament Mom had crocheted for the wreath had fallen to the ground. I picked it up and wiped off the dust and hay.

"No more treats until you say you're sorry."

Fire tossed his head. His forelock flopped down over his eyes, and I swear his lips curved up in a smile.

"You know you're too adorable to get mad at, don't you?"

Except for Robert and Luis and me, the barn was empty. The afternoon group lessons had been canceled for Christmas Eve, and only the beautiful sounds of horses and Christmas music floated gently down the aisle. I wove a piece of baling twine into the frame and hung the wreath on the wall where Fire couldn't reach it anymore, then cleaned up the mess. Every time I bent to sweep glitter and broken peppermints into the dustpan, he nibbled the back of my jacket.

"Stop!" I said, slapping the air in front of his face. "This jacket is practically brand-new! If you bite a hole in it, I'm telling Kennedy you're getting too much grain. Bad pony."

I pushed his muzzle away and kept sweeping.

"Hey!" Bryce ran toward us, his face stern. "Can you help me? I'm late for my dressage lesson!"

The barn door rolled partway open at the other end of the aisle. Mr. McDaid's silhouette loomed large and intimidating against a gray sky outside. His voice boomed.

"I'll be back at sixteen hundred hours, son. You be ready!"

Bryce jerked around and scowled at his father. "That doesn't leave me any time to cool Tucker out and put everything away!"

Mr. McDaid looked at his watch. "An extra five minutes, then. We're expected at Christmas Eve service at seventeen hundred. Be sure you give little Lizzie our message!"

Mr. McDaid saluted me and left. He always saluted, like he was in the army or something.

"What message?" I asked.

Bryce clipped Tucker to the cross-ties. "Can you not ask questions right now and just help? Kennedy said if I'm late again she won't teach me." His cheeks puffed up under watery eyes. It looked like he'd been crying just before he arrived. "I swear when he knows it's dressage day, my dad drives slower than a possum crossing the highway."

"I'll help," I said. "Give me a brush."

He handed me a rubber currycomb and together we speed-groomed Tucker. Within seven minutes, Tucker's coat gleamed, his hooves were picked, and he was tacked up and ready to go. Even so, Bryce didn't look any less grim. I gave Fire a peppermint, then followed Bryce into the ring and perched on top of the mounting block, my usual place where I sat to watch his lessons. Bryce tightened Tucker's girth, then warmed him up on a loose rein. With each step the horse took, Bryce's body softened. He was in his happy place again.

Kennedy bustled in. "I brought you a hot chocolate from my dad's pub," she said, holding out one of the green paper coffee cups with the peach-and-gold rose etched on the side, right above where it said *O'Toole's*. Every time she brought coffee in one of those cups, I remembered the roses blooming in the garden the day we left our old house. It was hard to believe it had been six whole months since then. It was impossible to believe it had been almost a year since I'd spoken to Dad.

I sipped the hot drink, grateful for its sweetness, for the warmth of the cup in my cold hand, and for Kennedy's voice as she started teaching Bryce and Tucker and me, on my first Christmas Eve without my father.

"You want to feel Tucker's inside hind leg engaging," Kennedy said.

For almost an hour, she walked in circles, following Bryce around the ring, her head tilted to one side as she studied him. Bryce's face went from stern concentration to flickers of a smile to a furrowed brow again. He'd told me how important it was to him to be perfect, because he wanted to ride in the Olympics someday.

"That inside hind leg should be moving on the same track as his outside front. That's right, that's good. Let his body bend, softly bend."

With each precise step, Tucker's muscles tightened, then relaxed, tightened, then relaxed, a combination of softness and strength. His neck arched and bent toward the inside, and his ears flicked back and forth. Bryce sat tall and straight-backed in the saddle, his stirrups long and his fingers flexing the reins. When Tucker suddenly got the movement exactly right, his whole body softened and a smile broke out on Bryce's face.

Kennedy raised her coffee cup in the air. "Yes! You felt it, right?"

"Yeah," Bryce said.

He moved his focus to his fingers holding the reins.

"Don't look down, Bryce. You'll lose your concentration. Eyes up! *Feel* his mouth in your hands; *feel* him chewing the bit. You have to learn to feel all this as if you were blindfolded."

They moved around the perimeter of the ring a few more times, such a beautiful unit of horse-and-human, it made chills travel all the way to my core.

"Nicely done," Kennedy said. "That's enough work for today. Let him stretch his neck. Give him a chance to think about grassy meadows while you cool him out."

Bryce let the reins slide through his fingers and took his feet out of the stirrups. His face glistened with sweat, but I knew his heart was happy. I knew because that's exactly how I would feel, too.

Sometimes, on the nights after I watched his lessons, I'd wait for Mom to go crochet with Mrs. Ivanov, and I'd stand in the small block of space between the end of the bunk beds and the window and pretend I was riding Fire, practicing my own perfect dressage movements. Other times, I'd lie in bed and let my imagination take us outside the ring. I dreamed about riding Fire bareback, crouched low over his neck with his long mane laced between my fingers as we galloped across open fields in the moonlight. In my imagination, we kept going on and on forever because there was nothing to stop us. Because we were free.

Kennedy sat down on a jump rail and finished off her coffee. "Well, Miss Lessons-with-Joe, how are they going? The lessons, I mean."

"Good," I said.

"They should be. Not many working students get to ride with him. They're usually stuck with me. You must be exceptional."

I'd heard another working student say she wished she could have lessons with Joe like me. I'd felt uneasy, almost embarrassed, but when I told Bryce, he said for me to ignore her and be grateful Joe had taken me on.

"I'm changing my diagonal on figure eights," I said, "and trotting over ground poles in the half-seat position. Next week I'm supposed to canter."

Kennedy raised her eyebrows. "Ooooh, the first canter. That's a big step. You are learning fast."

"I need to learn faster. I want to ride Fire as soon as I can."

Kennedy crushed the paper cup and stuffed it into the cardboard tray. "Yeah, everyone wants to ride Fire except me." She looked down and crossed her long legs at the ankles. "I'm not much for my feet dragging on the ground. If I ever get my own horse, it'll have to be at least sixteen hands, probably more."

"Yeah, he's definitely not tall enough for you."

She looked at me from the corner of her eye. "You should

know that since Fire's training has been going so well, people have been asking about buying him."

"Who?"

"Sabrina's dad for one. Look, Lizzie, just keep working hard in your lessons so maybe Joe will at least let you ride him. Once Fire's ready, he'll sell fast."

Sabrina!

Kennedy tapped my knee and frowned. "I'm sorry. I've been in your shoes a dozen times over the years. It is the worst. But you might as well know up front what's going to happen, instead of getting your hopes up and having your heart get broken over and over like mine always did."

She and Joe didn't know my plan. They didn't know that I was going to earn the money and buy Fire myself. If they knew, they'd wait for me.

"But I'm—"

Kennedy jumped up, cutting off my words. "Sorry, kiddo, I gotta go. My dad's waiting. Have a nice Christmas, okay?"

She gave me a one-arm hug, then waved at Bryce on her way out.

"Good work today, buddy. Merry Christmas!"

Bryce lifted his chin and smiled. "Thanks, you too!"

I was still sitting on the mounting block, trying to catch my breath, when he brought Tucker to the middle of the ring and dismounted.

"You don't look very merry," he said. "What's up?"

"Nothing."

He loosened the girth and threw a sheet over Tucker. "Come with me while I cool him out. Talk to me. I know something's wrong."

We led Tucker a few times around the ring before I said anything. "Are you still doing the hot-walking thing at the polo club?"

"Every Friday night."

"And you make money?"

"Yeah, a lot."

"Can I go with you?"

"Sure! It starts up again the first Friday in January. That'd be great."

"Okay, thanks."

My breath came a little easier. I had a plan. I could make it work.

"It will be fun, and I need to save money," I said cautiously.

I was giving him a chance to ask me what I was saving for, so I could decide how much to tell him. Before he could say anything, Mr. McDaid's big voice boomed through the barn.

"Son! Where are you?"

Bryce whipped around to face the gate. His eyes flashed. "Dang! I forgot about church. Now I'll be in for it!"

He shoved his hand under the cooler to feel Tucker's chest and shook his head.

"He's too hot. I can't put him away yet."

Mr. McDaid's footsteps pounded on the concrete. "Bryce!

Where are you? We're LATE!"

"Won't he wait?"

Bryce shook his head. "He's looking for reasons to take my dressage lessons away. I don't know what to do."

I grabbed the lead rope. "Go! I'll cool him out and put him away. Hurry!"

"You sure?"

"Boy!" Mr. McDaid bellowed.

"I'm positive. Go."

"Thanks, Lizzie, I owe you!" He sprinted away toward the barn. "Coming!"

Tucker and I stood in the middle of the suddenly silent ring, his breath still coming hard and hot. I could hear Robert and Luis throwing hay into the stalls from the loft overhead and the restless hum of horses waiting for their dinner.

A minute later, Bryce was back. "I forgot I was supposed to invite you and your mom for dinner tomorrow. Can you come?"

"Dinner? Where?"

"At my house, duh. Give me your mom's phone number. I'll have my dad call her."

He typed Mom's cell number into his phone, then clicked it off and waved.

"Gotta go. Thanks again, bye!"

Mr. McDaid's Escalade roared to life in the driveway. I waved to the sound of tires spinning, then gripping the gravel tossed over the ice, and the car sped off with a crunch.

* * *

Mom pulled her light blue sweater over her head and draped it across the back of the chair to dry out. Tiny crystals of snow dissolved into the weave of fabric.

"Boy, do I ever miss a fireplace," she said.

She stood thoughtfully in the middle of our tiny room, then shook her shoulders like she wanted to rid herself of a bad memory.

"Bryce's dad called. Did you know we were invited there for dinner tomorrow?"

I peeked over the rail of my bunk. I'd been in bed ever since I slipped in the back door mere seconds before Miss May traipsed down the hall to lock it.

"Sort of. He told me, then ran off with his dad to go to church. Are we going to church this year?"

She picked up the sweater from the chair, felt the fabric, then laid it over the back again and smoothed it with her fingers. "I don't know. I guess I forgot. Everything's so different. I could find a place to go if you want."

I turned away and stared at the ceiling. "I don't really care. Maybe next year."

Mom got busy doing what she did when something felt unpleasant or out of her control: she moved things around in the tiny closet. It was a weird habit she'd started when we first got to Good Hope and she couldn't make all our clothes fit in the tiny dresser. Finally, she sat down on the bed and rustled around inside a bag she'd brought home. I knew there were presents in there. I wished she hadn't spent the money. I wished I had the courage to ask her to save it and help me buy Fire.

"Did Dad send us anything for Christmas?" I asked. "Like money?"

There was a long pause before her phone beeped from the windowsill. Without answering me, she flipped it open and read the message.

"It's from Mr. McDaid," she said. "Bryce's dad. Do you want to go?"

"Do you?"

"If you do."

Staying at Good Hope for Christmas would mean having dinner brought in from the same church people who'd given us our Thanksgiving dinner. At Thanksgiving, Mom had reminded me to act grateful when I'd shrunk under their looks of pity, not wanting to eat. Going to the McDaids' would mean dealing with the awkward tension between Bryce and his dad, but it would probably be better than those pitiful looks.

"If we went, how would we get there?"

"Mr. McDaid said he would pick us up."

"No!" I said. "I don't want them coming here. Bryce doesn't know."

Mom startled, then laid the phone on the windowsill and sat on her bunk. "Lizzie, there is no shame in needing help from time to time. That's all we're doing here: getting a little extra help until we're back on our feet."

"It isn't about Good Hope exactly," I said. "It's about *why* we're here."

My words hung in the air.

Finally, Mom said, "If Bryce is a true friend, he'll know that what Dad did isn't our fault."

"Then why does it still feel like it?"

The quiet that followed was not the kind that had lifted our spirits on walks through the woods. It was the kind of quiet that rose into a barrier between us. I turned to face the wall, wishing it was already December 26 and that this first miserable Christmas on our own was over.

Finally, Mom stood up and patted my arm. "Come on, let's get dinner and make a decision on full stomachs. I think I saw some giant cans of Chef Boyardee ravioli on the counter. No matter what, we are not going to bed hungry on Christmas Eve."

The phone buzzed again as I was climbing down the ladder.

"It's Joe," Mom said. "Look."

She held the phone up for me to see his message.

WANT A RIDE TO THE MCDAIDS? I CAN PICK YOU UP AT NOON.

"Why is his message all in caps?"

Mom giggled. "Maybe he's one of those people who doesn't know how to text."

"Does Joe know about Dad?"

Mom shook her head. "Not unless you told him. He knows where we live, but he never asked why."

"Then can we ride to the McDaids' with him? I do want to go. I'm just not ready to tell Bryce why we live here."

She put her hand on the back of my neck and pulled me close, kissing the top of my head. "Of course we can, Lizzie. Let's go to the McDaids'. We'll start our own new traditions tomorrow."

FIFTEEN

Back home, in our life before Good Hope, Santa always left a stocking on my bed to open on Christmas morning. The stuff inside was supposed to keep me busy until I was allowed to wake up Mom and Dad. There were always oranges and whole nuts, then sometimes pencils and miniature Sudoku books or Silly Putty. The year we were ten, MaryBeth saw my stocking and told me all that stuff was dumb. Then she showed me the new purple iPod that came in her stocking, along with a fifty-dollar iTunes gift card. When I'd complained to Mom, she shut me down quickly.

"It's an old-fashioned family tradition," she'd said.

Before Good Hope, we had lots of traditions. Like every Christmas Eve, Mom read snow poems while Dad and I baked cookies for Santa and hung the stockings. Every Christmas morning, Mom was up early cooking homemade waffles and creamed chipped beef that we'd drown in real Vermont maple syrup.

"In honor of Granddad, who ate this every Christmas when he was fighting for our country in the navy," she'd say. "But he wasn't lucky enough to have syrup."

At dinner, each of our places would have those tube-shaped Christmas crackers wrapped in shiny paper and filled with tiny candies and toys that scattered all over the table when we pulled them apart.

"In honor of your Scottish heritage," Dad always said.

I had no idea what to expect this year. I knew what *not* to expect: piles of presents; Christmas waffles; Mom's roast beef; sparkling cider in champagne flutes; sledding on Powder Hill; and most of all, Dad. So when I opened my eyes a little after seven and felt the red crocheted stocking pushing against my foot, I almost cried. Tradition had triumphed.

Inside was a single orange, a little package of cashews, a miniature journal covered in aqua fabric, a purple pen, and a bunch of tiny hand-crocheted hearts. I sat by the window and wrote in the journal, hoping to capture the way it felt to watch the sky blush as the sun crested the top of the hill on

Christmas morning. I wrote without looking down, my eyes strained to examine the exact way light broke through the bare branches and reflected off the snow, turning everything pink, punctuated by black-capped chickadees darting from limb to limb, looking for food.

The chickadees were hungry. I'd never found that mother dog again, but there was something I could do to help the birds. Very quietly, I reached under Mom's bunk, where the bird feeder had lived ever since we'd moved to Good Hope. Opening the window, I pushed the feeder out, then slid the window shut again before the chill spread through the room. A roll of green yarn lay on top of Mom's crochet basket. I snipped a long piece to hang the feeder, wrote a quick note, and tiptoed out into the hallway.

The threat of Miss May's authority hadn't lessened in the six months we'd been at Good Hope. I found her in the kitchen stirring a big wooden spoon in a pot on the stove.

"Hello?"

She spun around so fast the spoon flew from her hand and bounced across the floor, splattering brown dots on olive-green linoleum.

"Elizabeth!" she yelped. "How many times have I told you not to startle me like that?"

"I'm sorry," I said, with as much remorse as I could muster for something I had never been told before. "I didn't mean— I was looking for the book to sign out. Oh, and I wanted to tell you Merry Christmas."

She stared at me like I was talking gibberish. Finally, she picked up the spoon and held her other hand underneath so whatever the brown stuff was made a pool in her palm.

"I'm Jewish," she said sharply.

"Oh. I'm sorry. I didn't know."

"It's not a disease, Elizabeth. It's a belief system."

"Yes, I know. I'm sorry. I just, well, you decorated the tree in the common room and all, so I assumed."

"I do it every year. For the residents. Always have." She puckered her lips and lifted her chin so she could look down her nose at me. "I, too, have a heart, Elizabeth."

"Oh, of course. I never—I mean—gosh, that's really nice—I mean, um, Happy Hanukkah?"

Miss May sighed. "Hanukkah ended two weeks ago."

"Oh. Right."

Seconds ticked by. Miss May rinsed the spoon and wiped up the drops on the floor with a paper towel. Then she turned back to the stove.

"Is that all you wanted?"

"Yes, well, no. I left Mom a note. I'm going out in the snow, just in the backyard, like to the bench, just for a little bit. It's so pretty. I thought I should let you know."

She nodded without saying a word. I didn't wait another breath before escaping out the back door.

Grabbing the bird feeder from where it had landed in the snow, I zigzagged my way across the yard, leaving a trail of footprints behind. I knew exactly where I was going to hang it: right in the thickest boughs on the back side of the cedar tree, out of sight of the kitchen window. After it was secured to the branch, I filled the base with sections of my orange and the cashews. Then I danced off into the woods, completely ignoring my promise to stay in the yard.

Cloven hoofprints crossed the trail near the bend, threading a new course deep into a labyrinth of trees. I pushed saplings and holly branches aside to follow the deer until, in the middle of that sleeping forest, I paused, listening to the perfect hush of stillness.

A buck turned his head and caught my eye. If he hadn't moved, he would have blended with the trees and I would have completely missed him. His antlers rose high above his head, with points spread like branches. He studied me with steady, dark eyes. He wasn't afraid. He was the master of these woods. He had ownership here. I breathed icy air deep into my lungs and hoped I could inhale some of that power.

The buck and the faint scent of birch reminded me of sitting on my grandparents' porch in Vermont and watching deer eat leaves and twigs in their yard. My grandparents' whose ashes were still buried under the red maple tree at our old house. Someday, I vowed, someday I'd have the power to go back and get them.

A cardinal broke the quiet with its noisy chatter. The buck turned away and disappeared into the endless white and gray, and I started for home.

* * *

Keeping secret the Christmas gift I'd made for Mom had been so hard, it was almost torture. But when she lifted white sparkly tissue away from the wrapping and drew in a breath, it was completely worth it. She traced the tip of her finger along each word of my poem that I'd written in calligraphy.

"Oh, Lizzie," she said, "I love it."

"Read the card," I said, handing her the tiny white envelope.

"'This poem I wrote for you, "Behind Birchwood," has been published in the winter edition of the high school newspaper and has also been entered into a poetry contest through the library.'"

Her hand went to her mouth. "Oh, sweetie, a budding equestrian and now you're a published poet, too! You are so amazing."

"I hope you like it. I wrote it in the fall. Ms. Fitzgerald gave me the matting, and she said she'd have a copy of the newsletter for me when school starts after the break. And if I win the contest, I get twenty-five dollars."

"Oh, my, and what would you do with that twenty-five dollars?"

It would be the middle of February before I knew if I won the money. That might be too late to help me buy Fire, especially if people kept asking to buy him.

"I don't know," I said.

"Hey, will you read the poem?" She closed her eyes and rested her back against the wall.

"It feels weird reading my own poem out loud to someone else."

"Do it anyway," she whispered. "For me."

Behind Birchwood

I dance around slippery rocks
blanketed in deep green moss,
jump last year's logs, rotted
now and slick with earth.
Raindrops ping in a slow,
steady rhythm, dropping
onto holdout leaves still
clinging to near-bare
limbs. Water trickles
in rivulets down
skinny spines,
gathers in tiny
puddles, cupped
in wet clumps
of decayed
leaves on
the ground,
soon to be
covered by
frost, then
hidden
under
snow.

Change is near.

Mom's lips curved up into a soft smile.

"That's my favorite part," she said. "Change is near."

SIXTEEN

Joe listened to Christmas music in the car on the way to the McDaids'. That surprised me almost as much as Mr. McDaid's house did—it was sunshine-yellow with hundreds of white lights circling the pillars out front. He even had a life-sized baby Jesus by the front door, all tucked into a manger strung with more lights alongside Mary, Joseph, and all three of those kings. None of it matched Mr. McDaid's abrasive personality.

"Holy mackerel, so fancy," Mom said. She smoothed the collar over her blue sweater. "I'm not sure we're dressed appropriately."

I tugged my denim skirt down over black leggings and flinched. It was all I had, except one super-dressy dress that I hadn't worn in over a year. Joe loosened his tie and pulled it off.

"You're dressed perfectly. I'm overdressed. You'll see." He tossed the tie into the back seat next to me and smiled. "And you look almost like a regular girl in that skirt, Lizzie. Barely any trace of horse-girl at all."

We walked up a brick path to the house and stood beside the manger. A string of lights on the edge had fallen and lay across baby Jesus's face. The lights twinkled, and Jesus winked at me. Right when I started to giggle, Bryce flung the door open.

"Come on in," he said, waving us into a two-story foyer with cream-and-turquoise marble floors.

Another surprise. I didn't know what I expected, but it wasn't this. Mr. McDaid barreled in, his face ruddy as if he'd been outside in a cold wind all day. He pushed Bryce aside to get to us.

"Merry Christmas! Merry Christmas!"

He pumped Joe's hand like he was trying to squeeze the last bit of water from a well. Joe put his other hand under Mom's elbow.

"Michael, this is Isabel, Lizzie's mom."

Mr. McDaid stood up tall, inhaled deeply, and puffed his chest out. "Well, now, you are just as lovely as your daughter."

"Oh, well, thank you, Mr. McDaid—" Mom said.

"Ach! No, no! It's Michael. Michael to all of you!"

He opened his arms wide and came at us like he wanted a group hug. I shrank away, saved from being crushed in an awkward embrace by Bryce pulling me out of the circle.

"Dad, stop! You're weirding her out!" he said, scowling. "Come on, Lizzie, I'll show you Tucker's trophy room."

I gladly followed him away.

Bryce's house made me think about shoes. Like when you have an old pair that is too tight, but you wear them every day anyway and don't realize how squished and painful your toes are until you slip your feet into new shoes that fit and suddenly your feet can spread out and breathe again. Bryce's house was a new pair of shoes. The hallways were wide enough for me to hold both arms straight out at my sides and spin around like Julie Andrews in *The Sound of Music* if I wanted to. The furniture was pristine, as if no one ever sat on it, and every room had sunny floor-to-ceiling windows. There wasn't one dark corner. It was so different from Good Hope.

Tucker's trophy room was on the second floor, with a gold nameplate bolted right smack in the middle of the door. *Nip N Tuck*, it said in script. Inside, the room was lined wall to wall with shelves of trophies and photographs.

"Take a look," Bryce said. "I have to do something real quick."

He dropped into a purple velvet beanbag chair and flipped open his laptop. I looked away and moved slowly around the room, studying the pictures while he typed. When the typing paused, I pointed to a picture of him and Tucker against a backdrop of snowcapped mountains.

"Is this where you lived?"

"Yup," he said, studying the computer screen.

"Did you ride in the mountains?"

"All the time."

"What's this one?"

Bryce glanced up. "Me and Tucker roping. First time we won. My dad decided that meant I was a manly man, so he had it blown up extra big, like we lived in Texas or something."

In the picture Tucker was racing across an arena with his body low to the ground, his ears back, and his eyes focused on a terrified little red calf running away from him. Bryce was leaning forward over the pommel of a heavy western saddle, swinging the thick loop of a rope in the air.

"So weird seeing Tucker in a western saddle instead of your dressage one," I said.

"Night and day. Clunk and grace," Bryce grumbled.

"I knew you rode western, but I didn't know you did rodeo kind of stuff."

"My dad made me."

"You didn't like it?"

"It's . . . no big deal. The picture I really want is of us winning in dressage, but if my dad has his way, that'll never happen."

I sat cross-legged on the floor next to him. "Why not?"

"We fight about it all the time. That's why he was all pumped up when you guys got here. He was yelling at me again."

"About what?"

Bryce's face got really tight, and his jaw made this clicking sound.

"He says boys who ride dressage are gay. I have an older brother from when my dad was married before. Winston. He's gay. He lives in Oregon. I've seen him only three times in my whole life and only because my mom convinced him to come to a few of my birthday parties when I was little."

"Where is your mom?"

"Wyoming. That's who I was just messaging."

"Is she moving here?"

He shook his head. "They're divorced."

"Your dad got custody?"

"No, I got to pick. I would have stayed with my mom, but we live so far out in the mountains, it's near impossible to find dressage trainers who will travel to give me lessons. When my dad came here, he promised to bring Tucker and let us get trained. I believed him, so my mom and I decided I should come. Now he has all these stipulations."

"Like what?"

He slammed the laptop shut and swiped hair from his forehead. "If I don't do this or that, I don't get my lesson. He says he never promised I could show Tucker in dressage, only that I could learn. He's a jerk and a bully and I hate him."

"I'm really sorry. Maybe if he saw how good you two are."

"It doesn't matter. He won't come watch."

"Can you go back to Wyoming?"

"Ha! He'd never pay for Tucker to be shipped home, and my mom can't afford it. She'd sell everything she's got to make it happen if I asked, but I can't let her do that."

"So you have to choose between going home or keeping Tucker?"

"I'm not leaving my horse. My mom understands. Someday I might have to ride him the two thousand miles to get home, but for now I'm trapped."

The sad, sweet notes from "O Holy Night" floated upstairs and trapped me in a memory of Christmas music coming from Dad's study. I'd been trying really hard not to think about him all day. Every time I let my mind wander in that direction, it felt like something was sweeping me toward a big black hole.

"I'm trapped, too," I blurted.

Bryce's eyes darted in my direction, but he didn't say anything. Neither of us did for the rest of the song. When it was finished, he shifted in the beanbag.

"Do you want to sit here? The floor isn't very comfortable."

"I'm okay."

I picked at a loose thread along the hem of my skirt.

"Are your parents divorced?" Bryce asked.

"No," I said. "I mean, I don't think so. I never asked."

"Did they have custody hearings?"

"I'm not really sure."

"If they did, they're probably divorced."

"I don't think they can get a divorce," I said. "At least not until—"

I stopped. Bryce scrunched his forehead and waited. My eyes burned and my face turned hot all the way to the tips of my ears.

"My dad's in jail," I said, unraveling another piece of thread. "I mean, he was in jail. He has to have a trial."

Bryce didn't flinch. "That's ugly," he said.

But that was all. He didn't ask why Dad was in jail. He didn't make me say anything else, even though he must have known I had more secrets, the same way I knew he did, too.

Downstairs, the doorbell rang.

SEVENTEEN

A minute later, the door to the trophy room opened and Kennedy stuck her head inside.

"Hey, guys! Merry Christmas! Can I come in?"

"Of course!" Bryce perked up. "Look at you, all fancy with earrings and everything."

She flipped her fingertips across the top of his head and sat down so the three of us made a triangle. "Oh, shut up, it's once a year. Lizzie, you look nice. Not every day one gets invited to a palace, huh? Have you ever been here before?"

I shook my head.

"Well, it's always an interesting experience, right, Bryce?"

He snorted. Kennedy held up two packages wrapped in brown paper cut from a horse-feed bag, each one tied with a piece of hay string.

"So, guess who gets which one?"

Bryce put his hand out. "Give it over."

Kennedy tossed one to him, then held out the other to me. "And this is for you."

"Oh," I said. "I didn't know you were coming. I didn't even know *we* were coming until last night or I would have brought something—"

"Lizzie, *stop*!" Kennedy tapped the package. "Don't take the pleasure of giving a gift away from me."

Bryce rolled his eyes and grinned. "Yeah, Lizzie. Don't be so mean."

"Open!"

Kennedy had taken "before" and "after" photos of both of us and put them in double frames. On the left side of my frame was a picture taken last summer, long before I knew Kennedy. Long before I knew that she knew me. I was lying on my belly at the edge of the pastures, the rich, green grass all around me. My dark hair fell in an unruly mess at my shoulders, like maybe I hadn't even taken the time to brush it before running off through the woods to the horse farm that day. A pencil in my hand hovered over the pages of a notebook, but my eyes were trained on something far away on the hill.

On the right side of the frame was a more recent picture

of me walking away from the camera. I was wearing the paddock boots Joe had given me, and I was hauling a full bale of hay down the aisle, my back strained under the weight. My hair was pulled into a ponytail with a few pieces of straggly hay tagging along, and the seat of my jeans had dust from where I'd been sitting on the floor outside Fire's stall.

I pointed to the first one. "How'd you get this?"

"I'm a photography major," she said. "I have to know when and where to get the best pictures. These are two of my favorites I've ever taken. The evolution of Lizzie St. Clair."

I touched the image of the girl I'd been this summer and instantly felt the loneliness I'd walked around with for so many months. In the second picture, the loneliness was all but gone. Kennedy had watched me change, and she wanted me to know. She wanted me to step into the new pair of shoes and breathe.

The three of us were called down for dinner a few minutes later. There was a new person sitting in the living room next to Mom: a tall, handsome black man in a cream wing chair, his chin on his fist, his eyes pinned on Mom's face. He was listening to her talk like no one else existed in the entire universe.

"Hey, Dad," Kennedy said.

He startled and stood up. "Oh, hi, honey!"

"Dad, this is Lizzie." Kennedy pushed me toward him. "Lizzie, my dad, Jamie O'Toole."

Jamie was wearing a crisp white button-down shirt with

the sleeves rolled up. Over the left pocket, the signature O'Toole's Pub rose was embroidered in peach and gold. He stood up and reached a hand out to shake mine.

"So nice to meet you, Lizzie. I have to say, I didn't make the connection that the Lizzie Kennedy always talked about was the same Lizzie as Isabel's daughter."

I looked at Kennedy with her pale skin, long blond hair, and clear blue eyes, then to Jamie with his dark skin, black hair cropped close to his head, and dark eyes. He had to be her stepfather.

Mom leaned forward in her chair. "O'Toole's Pub is next door to my office. We have our lunch meetings there every week. Jamie and I met this fall."

"This fall?"

Kennedy nudged me with her elbow. "Cool."

Jamie smiled at Mom in a way that made me feel like a hummingbird was whizzing around inside my stomach.

"Yes, I know your mom from the pub. But I didn't imagine she'd be here today. What a surprise. A lovely surprise."

"Yeaaaah, how 'bout that?" Kennedy nudged me again. "Who knew?"

I didn't know what to do with my hands, or my feet, or my eyes. I couldn't look at Mom—but I had to look at Mom. She was smiling at me, and she was blushing.

"Jamie's the one who taught me how to crochet," she said.

Jamie rocked back on his heels and smiled. "I did, indeed."

That's when I noticed the gray-and-navy scarf lying over

the arm of the chair he'd been sitting in. The same gray-and-navy yarn Mom had in her basket at home. She knew him well enough to make him a scarf and hadn't even told me.

Joe burst through a swinging door from the kitchen wearing a shiny red crown that said *Merry Christmas* on it and carrying a tray of round things wrapped in foil.

"Hot baked potatoes," he said cheerfully, crossing the room. "This way to dinner, folks!"

I was still stunned when we all moved together into the dining room. Kennedy pulled out a chair across from where Mom and Jamie went to sit.

"Stay here with me and Bryce," she said firmly, pushing my shoulder and guiding me into the seat.

Mr. McDaid came in, balancing a platter on one hand and hoisting a giant grilling fork in the air with the other. "Oh, you are going to love this."

He made his way around the table and slapped pieces of meat onto everyone's plates. When he was done, he dropped the tray onto a sideboard, yanked out his chair, and sat down to eat Christmas dinner with a bloodied apron still tied around his body. He pointed his knife at each of us.

"Go ahead, go ahead, dig in, folks. Get a potato. Bryce, be polite. Pass those green beans around. No meat sauce needed for this meal. Elk is the finest red meat there is," he said. "Shot this bull myself in the fall when I went back to Wyoming to hunt with my buddies. Got him right between the eyes."

He pushed his index finger into the dip above the bridge of his nose to make sure we had a visual of exactly where that elk had been shot. I shuddered and looked at the barely dead thing on my plate.

"Should we say grace first?" Jamie asked.

Mr. McDaid stopped with his fork poised to sink into the meat. "Grace? Oh, yes, of course, please say grace."

He set his silverware down and propped his elbows on the table, his hands clasped together. The rest of us bowed our heads while Jamie recited a short, polite prayer. I didn't even hear what he said, really, because all I could think of was Kennedy saying, *It's always an interesting experience.*

"Amen," Jamie said.

"Amen," we echoed.

Mom's forehead gathered into little wrinkles above her eyes when she sliced into her meat. I watched her eat it. She even smiled as if she liked it, but I couldn't touch mine. Blood seeped into a puddle on my plate. Every time I started toward it with my fork, I thought of the buck I'd seen in the woods that morning. I was grateful to be invited for Christmas dinner, but I wasn't going to touch that poor dead elk.

Mr. McDaid pointed his fork at Bryce. "You eat that, son. None of this vegetarian stuff on Christmas. Not when I shot that thing just for you." He looked around at each of us with a grin that made me shiver. "My boy thinks he wants to be a vegetarian, like some kind of tree hugger. Can't grow up strong without protein, right, Joe?"

Joe cut into his meat and nodded, but when Mr. McDaid wasn't watching, he winked at Bryce. Mr. McDaid guzzled three glasses of champagne, one right after the other, and talked nonstop. He was kind of like Jenna in my English class: he talked all about himself. When the champagne bottle was empty, he went off to the kitchen for another one. Joe quickly switched out the bare bone from the chop he'd already eaten with the one Bryce wasn't going to touch. In the same breath, Kennedy grabbed mine and dropped her bone onto my plate.

"Thank you," I whispered.

"Teamwork," she said under her breath.

By the time Mr. McDaid came back, we were all happily enjoying our meal.

It was nearing dark when Mom and I piled into Joe's car to go home. I leaned my head against the window in the back seat, holding the framed photos in one hand. With the other, I caressed the arm of the brand-new pink Birchwood jacket Mr. McDaid had given me. Something about getting such an extravagant gift from someone I barely knew felt wrong, like maybe Mr. McDaid was trying to make me ignore the fact that he was mean to Bryce.

Mom loosened the new cashmere scarf he'd given her and waved out the window at Jamie, who was standing next to baby Jesus and waving back. Just before we turned the corner, Jamie stepped on the lit frame of Mary and Joseph, and the entire front of the house went dark. Joe, Mom, and I all three giggled.

"Kennedy's dad is nice," I said when we pulled onto the parkway.

"Yes, very," Mom said.

"So are you dating him?"

Joe chuckled and tapped the rearview mirror. "Hey, not to change the subject, but awesome gift from Mr. McDaid, huh?"

I ran my fingers across the bumpy threads where my name was embroidered in script on the front of my jacket. "Yeah. But do you think I should keep it?"

"Why would you not keep it?" Joe asked.

"I don't know. It just feels like a bribe or something."

"My, my, so judge-y," Mom said over her shoulder.

"Mr. McDaid is complicated. He's really loud, and he shoots elk between the eyes and serves it up for Christmas dinner, and tries to make Bryce feel ashamed for being a vegetarian, but then he does something like giving me the jacket."

"Well, it was very sweet to invite us and give such thoughtful gifts."

Joe nodded. "But you're right, Lizzie. He is a complex man, to be sure."

I drifted in and out of sleep until we pulled up in front of Good Hope and the car door light came on.

"I didn't get to see Fire today, Mom. It's Christmas. I

should have gone to see him."

"All is quiet at the barn now," Joe said. "You'll see him tomorrow."

"Yes, tomorrow," Mom said. "It's soon enough."

It was never soon enough. But I went inside without arguing, my fingers wrapped around the one-hundred-dollar bill that Mr. McDaid had tucked inside the pocket of my new jacket with a note that said, *To my new friend, Little Lizzie.* The note and the money made me feel even more uneasy. I wasn't sure what to do about it, but I put that bill into its own envelope, apart from the money I'd earned. I had plenty of time to decide.

"Mom?"

No answer. I'd fallen asleep on top of Mom's covers when we got home, still fully clothed. She had gone to crochet in the common room with Mrs. Ivanov, but now her jeans and sweater were draped over the chair and the curtain was closed.

"Mom?"

I tapped the underside of the mattress above me.

"Mom! Are you up there?"

"What is it? What time is it?"

"I don't know. Your phone's on the windowsill."

"It's late. Or early. Go back to sleep."

I could hear her turning over and wrestling with the covers.

"Mom?"

"What?"

"Can we talk?"

Silence.

More silence.

"Are you there?"

"Yes," she said. "I'm tired, but I'm here."

"Does that mean we can talk?"

"Sure, go for it."

"Are you and Dad divorced?"

"Why would you ask me that?"

"Because Bryce's parents are divorced, and he asked me if you and Dad were and I didn't know. He said there'd have been a custody hearing if you were getting divorced."

Pause.

"Well, there's been no custody hearing. You're stuck with me."

"I mean, you have reason to be divorced, right? After what Dad did?"

"I suppose so, sweetie, but why are you even thinking about that?"

"I was just wondering."

Silence.

"Mom?"

"Yes?"

"Do you *like*-like Jamie?"

I heard her push back her covers and sigh. "Since we're

awake, let's switch to our normal places. I'm getting vertigo up here."

She climbed down, but I didn't get out. I moved over against the wall and patted the empty side.

"Take your shoes off and I'll get in," Mom said.

I lifted my feet and giggled. "That's funny. I fell asleep with my shoes on."

Once I'd pushed them to the floor, we both crawled underneath the covers.

"This feels like my slumber party on my tenth birthday," I said, "when MaryBeth and Amy and Sloan and I slept in your bed."

Mom pulled the covers up to her chin. "Neither your dad nor I slept that night. Between the two of us scrunched together in your single bed, and all the giggling coming from the four of you in our room, it was a long night."

"It was fun, though. They all said it was the best birthday party they'd ever been to."

"I'm glad, Lizzie," she said. "Do you miss them? Your friends from back home?"

"Not really," I said. "I mean, I don't really think about them anymore. Besides, they weren't very nice to me after Dad left. They didn't act like real friends."

Mom reached over and squeezed my hand. "You've got Kennedy and Bryce now, and they both seem genuine and deserving of you."

"Mr. McDaid thinks Bryce is gay because he wants to

learn dressage. That's a type of riding."

"I know what dressage is. Why would that make him gay?"

"I don't know. Mr. McDaid is prejudiced, I guess."

"People who don't understand something that is different can be afraid of it. Sometimes it's their fear that turns into their prejudice."

"Do you think riding dressage could make someone just a little gay?"

"I don't think a person can be a little gay or a lot gay. I think they are, or they aren't. But then again, what do I know?"

I wondered about that for a second, about how Mom thought a person had to be either gay or not gay. Or a person had to be guilty or innocent. To her, it was black and white. No gray areas. But then why did it still feel like we were a little bit guilty for what Dad had done?

"Is he gay?" she asked.

"I'm not sure."

"Would it bother you if he was?"

"No."

"Good."

"Why?"

"Just checking to be sure I'm raising you right."

I nestled in closer to her. "Yeah, you are. Good night."

"Good night, my sweet Lizzie. Merry Christmas."

"Merry New Christmas, Mom. I love you."

EIGHTEEN

I laid Ben Franklin faceup on top of my covers. "One hundred five, one hundred ten, fifteen, twenty, thirty, thirty-five, fifty-five, sixty-five, eighty-five, ninety, two hundred, two hundred ten."

I stacked each of the bills I'd earned from babysitting on top of the hundred from Mr. McDaid, and wrote the new total in my notebook. I still wasn't sure how I felt about accepting the money from him, but every time I thought of Fire, I pushed that uneasy feeling to the back of my mind. Even with Mr. McDaid's gift, I needed another seven hundred and ninety dollars to reach my goal. Sometimes that number felt impossible, then other times I knew I could do it. In exactly one week, Bryce and I would go to hot-walk the horses at the indoor polo matches, and I'd have another way to earn money.

The shower water stopped in the bathroom. I shoved the notebook and money all together into the extra pillowcase I'd nabbed and pushed it between the wall and my mattress just before Mom came back in.

"Well, well," she said. She had a towel wrapped around her hair, which was all piled on top of her head. "The birthday girl is awake! Happy Birthday!"

"Thanks."

"How does it feel to be a teenager?"

"I dunno, same as it felt yesterday, I guess, and the day before and the day before that."

"Same as it did when you were six?"

I lay back and stared at a stain on the ceiling. "Probably different than when I was six. Remember that gigantic dollhouse you gave me for that birthday?"

"The one you promptly turned into a stable for your plastic horses?"

"Yeah." I grinned. "That one. But I never did get real hay to put in it like Dad promised."

"Well, people and promises, you know what they say about those, right?"

"No, what do they say?"

She rubbed her hair dry, then ran a comb through it and smiled at me in the mirror. "I don't really know what they say. I made that up."

"And here I thought you were going to say something meaningful."

"Spoken like a true teen," she said. "I'm sorry I can't be there for your canter lesson today, but we'll have a nice celebration tonight, okay?"

"No biggie. I didn't tell anyone it was my birthday anyway."

Everyone said my canter lesson was a huge step toward being a good rider. I needed to be more than a good rider. I needed to be the kind who deserved Fire, and I needed to get there fast. Every time I thought about this lesson, my belly flipped. I'd even asked Joe if we could have the lesson in the private ring so there wouldn't be anyone coming by and distracting me. Everything had to be perfect.

Later that morning, Joe met me and Rusty in the ring. He tucked his cell phone into his coat pocket and blew on both hands before putting his gloves back on.

"We picked a chilly day for this lesson," he said.

"My eyeballs felt like icicles by the time I got here."

"Good thing you've got that fancy new jacket to keep you warm. You excited to canter?"

My fingers automatically went to the arm of the pink

Birchwood jacket and touched the soft leather. It wasn't particularly warm, so I'd layered clothes underneath: T-shirt, turtleneck, and a sweatshirt. I tugged on the collar of the turtleneck and felt the rim of sweat already around the edge.

"Yeah, and a little nervous."

"Pshaw. Nervous? You've got this in spades."

"I know I can do it. I just need to do it really well."

Part of me hoped he would ask what I meant by *needing* to do it really well. Part of me really wanted to tell him about saving money for Fire, but another part of me held back.

"I wouldn't expect anything less," he said.

Rusty pushed his belly out when I pulled the girth up.

"Press your knee into his side," Joe said. "Make him let go of that air."

I got the girth buckled tight just as Sabrina and Rikki waltzed into the ring, their arms looped together. Joe looked at them suspiciously.

"What's up, girls?"

"Nothing," Rikki said. They sat side by side on the mounting block.

"Don't you have something to do?" Joe asked.

"No," Sabrina said.

"Not until our lesson later," Rikki said.

I gritted my teeth and mounted Rusty.

"Go ask Kennedy if she needs help in the barn, then," he said firmly. "This lesson is private."

Rikki tilted her head and pouted. "You always let us watch the working student lessons."

"Besides, she doesn't care. We go to school together, right, Lizzie?" Sabrina said.

My chest burned like someone had lit a fire inside. It was one thing to avoid making friends, but I didn't want anyone getting mad at me, either. I shrugged, then quickly maneuvered Rusty out of the middle of the ring and pushed him into a trot.

Up-down, up-down, up-down.

"Go, girls, out," Joe said firmly.

"Okay, but she's on the wrong diagonal," Rikki said.

I glanced down at Rusty's shoulders. She was right. My body rose out of the saddle when his *inside* leg moved forward instead of his outside leg. I'd never missed a diagonal before—ever.

"Thank you for bringing that to my attention," Joe said. "Now please leave so we can concentrate."

I clenched my teeth, sat one beat, and trotted on.

Up-down, up-down, up-down.

Rikki and Sabrina looped arms and trudged slowly across the ring toward the gate. They stalled near the edge so I had to trot through a narrow lane between them and the kickwall. I kept my eyes straight ahead.

Up-down, up-down, up-down.

Once they left, Joe told me to walk.

"Sorry about that intrusion," he said.

"It's okay." I wiped my face and wove my fingers through Rusty's scraggly mane.

"You know, they aren't bad girls," he said. "A bit on the busybody side, but I don't think they mean any harm."

I let the reins slip through my fingers so Rusty could put his head down and relax. I knew they weren't bad girls, and I knew in their weird way they were trying to be friendly toward me. But that was the problem. I couldn't handle friends right now. They wouldn't like me if they knew who I really was, and it was too much work to try to pretend to be someone else.

When I rode past the gate, I caught a glimpse of Rikki and Sabrina squatting on the back side of the kick-wall. They'd found a way to watch without Joe knowing. Sabrina put her hands up as if she was saying, *Please?* Rikki put her finger to her lips. I looked away and pretended I didn't see.

"Okay," Joe said. "Start your trot."

I pushed Rusty hard to get momentum going. *Up-down, up-down, up-down.* We went through two corners then down the long side. *Up-down, up-down, up-down.*

"Excellent," Joe said. "Now, get into your half seat."

I shortened my reins, pushed my heels down, and raised out of the saddle.

"Tell me about your position," he said.

"Chin up, eyes forward, shoulders over my knees, knees over my toes, weight in my heels, hands on both reins!"

"Good, now bring your shoulders back a little. And don't

grip with your knees. It's all about balance, remember?"

"Yup!"

"Tie up your reins and drop them on his neck, then put both your arms straight out to the side. Stay in your half-seat position."

I did as he said and felt the weight of my body sink farther into my heels. Rusty plodded along at a steady and safe pace through two more corners and another long stretch of the ring.

"Well done," Joe said. "Without looking down, pick your reins back up and untie them."

I lifted them from Rusty's bobbing neck, untied them, and tightened my hold until I could feel his mouth chewing the bit.

"Excellent, Lizzie. Very good. You ready?"

"Ready!"

My heart soared. I was going to canter.

"Tell me with words what aids to use."

I waited until we passed the spot where Rikki and Sabrina were peeking through the break in the kick-wall. "Outside leg behind the girth, inside leg on the girth, hold my outside rein and squeeze."

"Where are you going to do it?"

"Right before a corner."

"Which corner?"

"Whichever one you tell me."

"The next one!"

"What?"

"Canter now! Go, go, go!"

I put my legs in place and squeezed, but Rusty kept plodding along at the trot.

"Again! Harder!"

Rusty trotted faster but still no canter.

"Again!" Joe yelled.

This time, I used the secret trick Kennedy had shared with me and dug my outside heel into Rusty's side. As soon as my foot connected, the rhythm changed and we sailed into a beautiful, rocking canter.

One-two-three, one-two-three, one-two-three.

"You did it!"

We cantered through the next corners until the long side of the ring stretched out before me again.

One-two-three, one-two-three, one-two-three.

It was so easy, I wished now that Mom was here to watch.

"When you feel ready," Joe called, "lower yourself and sit. Nice and slow."

My heels sank. I moved my body back a tiny bit and settled into the saddle.

One-two-three, one-two-three, one-two-three.

"Your arms are flapping like chicken wings!"

I tucked my elbows against my sides, and my lips unfurled into a smile. The cold air hit my teeth, but I couldn't have stopped smiling if I tried. I was cantering, and I knew someday I'd canter Fire, too. One day when he and I were both fully trained, we'd canter up the hill in the same fields I'd watched horses gallop through all summer. We'd canter down the path in the woods, maybe go as far as Good Hope so I could show Angela's kids. Even Miss May might be impressed. And maybe Leonard wouldn't be sour and would finally smile at me. Fire and I would be a team. Connected. The perfect pair. More even than Tucker and Bryce. Kindred spirits.

BAM!

Rusty swerved sharply away from the burst of noise coming from behind the kick-wall. He threw his head down between his knees, yanked the reins out of my hands, and bucked. I lurched sideways, my hands flailing, my eye right next to Rusty's front leg when it rose and came back down with the reins tangled tightly around his fetlock. He crashed to his knees, sending a dark cloud of dirt up around him. I projected through the air and landed hard, flat on my back.

NINETEEN

Joe raced across the ring. "You okay?"

I rolled to my side and spit out dirt that tasted like metal. Blood. My lip was cut and bleeding.

"Whoa, whoa. Stay still. Don't move," Joe said. He put his hand gently on my shoulder to steady me. "Your lip is cut. Does anything else hurt?"

"I'm okay, just dizzy. Is Rusty okay?"

"Lie back for a second, Lizzie," he said. He pulled his coat off and made a pillow for my head. I closed my eyes and heard him go to where Rusty was breathing hard.

"Hold still, buddy. Let me just check your leg," he said.

"Is he okay?"

"There's a little swelling, but nothing feels out of place. He could have broken his leg in a fall like that."

"I'm sorry, Joe."

He came and helped me sit up, then stand on wobbly legs. My brand-new pink jacket was covered in dirt and spit, and a tiny clump of horse manure clung to the zipper. Every muscle in my body felt the way it had when I'd had the flu: sore, stretched, and beaten. Rusty watched me with forgiving eyes, his right front leg lifted completely off the ground.

"Can he walk?"

"Can you?" Joe asked. "Then we'll see about him."

"I'm okay."

Rusty wouldn't put any weight on the injured leg. With both of us hobbling, getting to the wash stall was a long process. Rusty limped along, one hoof, two hoof, three hoof, hop and stop. One hoof, two hoof, three hoof, hop and stop.

Joe turned over a large rubber bucket in the wash stall. "Sit there," he said.

I lowered myself gingerly while Joe stripped off Rusty's saddle. He turned on the overhead heater and let cool water dribble from the hose. His face was crimson, and his brows were all bunched up in the center of his forehead.

"He's pretty banged up," he said, eyeing the leg closely. "No lessons for him for a while. Hopefully he'll be okay after a few days' rest."

I touched the velvety end of Rusty's nose with my fingertip.

"I can pay for his medicine. I have money saved."

Joe poured sharp-smelling liniment onto a rag and rubbed it into Rusty's back.

"Don't think for one second I don't know why that happened," he said. "He'll be okay, you'll be okay, but it could have been worse. And it could have been prevented."

I swallowed hard, trying to hold in a giant sob rising in my chest. "I lost my balance when he spooked."

Joe squatted and gently touched Rusty's injured leg with the rag. "Easy, fella," he said. "Lizzie, you forget. I saw the whole thing, remember?"

I wished this miserable day was over and I could go back to our room, crawl under the covers, and start again tomorrow.

"This pony would never spook," Joe said. "It only happened because those girls banged on the wall."

"Wait, what?"

He ground up a white tablet and fed it to Rusty in a handful of sweet feed. "I don't know if it was an accident or not, but I'll be having a serious conversation with their parents."

I watched Joe's face to be sure I understood what he was saying.

"I thought you were mad at me."

"You? Why would I be mad at you? Have a little faith in yourself, Lizzie. You did nothing wrong."

Maybe Joe was right. Maybe I didn't have faith in myself anymore. I hadn't always been that way. I took the hose from him and pointed the stream of water at Rusty's knee.

"I can do this," I said.

"Good girl. Hose it for fifteen minutes, then give him a hot bran mash. I'm going to find Rikki and Sabrina."

He turned briskly, but I grabbed his arm. "Wait!"

"What?"

"Can you maybe not tell their parents?"

"Why would you want that? They've hurt one of our best school ponies and could have seriously injured you."

"It was a mistake. I'm sure of it. Maybe you can just give them a warning or something."

"Lizzie, if I don't talk to their parents, what kind of message does that send to them and all the other students who will hear about this? They need to understand how dangerous their actions were, and that there are consequences."

"I know, but I don't want them mad at me. They'll think I told you because I saw them. They just wanted to watch."

"Why didn't you say something?"

I shrugged but didn't answer. The truth was, I didn't want to cause any trouble. I wanted to be invisible. I wanted to fly solo, like Ms. Fitzgerald said. Get through until Mom and I lived someplace where she could just be a regular divorced mom with a job and where I wouldn't be the kid with a dad going to jail. If I gave these girls any reason to be mad at me—or to notice me at all—my life here was only going to get harder.

Joe watched me for a second and his whole expression softened. "I get why you didn't speak up, but I saw it myself."

"They'll still blame me. You know they will. And this is the only place I can—"

I stopped before my voice cracked. The smell of liniment made my eyes water. Joe and I watched dirty water swirl down the drain, washing away evidence of Rusty's fall. Neither one of us said anything for a couple of moments. Finally, he put his hand on my shoulder and turned me to face him.

"Okay, Lizzie, I understand. I really do. This is my safe place, too."

Then he left with his head down and hands stuffed in his coat pockets.

When I was done, I covered Rusty with a blanket and went to mix up the hot bran mash. The first time I'd made one, I'd gotten it all wrong, so Kennedy had written the recipe on the chalkboard in the feed room.

1 cup bran
½ cup oats
½ cup molasses
Chopped carrots, raisins, crushed peppermints,
whatever you have
Add lots of super-hot water until it is like thin soup.
Stir.

The warm, sweet smell rose from the bucket and made me long for a really good, homemade breakfast. Someday, it would be that way again.

Rusty slurped up the mash while I went to the loft and threw two flakes of hay into his stall. As soon as he was tucked away for the afternoon, I slipped into Fire's stall and wrapped my arms around his neck.

"It's my birthday, Fire," I said. "It doesn't feel like it. I mean, I didn't tell anyone on purpose, but it's weird. This is my first birthday without at least a cake. Maybe I'm too old for that stuff anyway."

Fire pushed his muzzle against my chest, telling me to scratch him.

"You're so predictable." I laughed. "The most predictable thing in my whole entire universe. We're in this together, you and me."

"Lizzie?"

I quickly wiped hay and shavings from my clothes and stepped out of the stall. Kennedy stood halfway up the aisle, her hands on her hips.

"Joe needs to see you in his office."

The way she said it worried me. Maybe Joe had changed his mind about calling Rikki's and Sabrina's parents. Or maybe both girls were in there and he was making them apologize to my face. Maybe I could just die.

I walked slowly toward the office, flip-flopping on what to say. What if their parents were there, too? I hesitated outside the door, but Kennedy came up behind me and gave a little nudge in my back.

"Just go," she said. "He doesn't bite."

"Why does he need to see me?"

"Who knows? Get it over with."

It was obvious she knew and wasn't going to tell me, which felt like she was stabbing me in the back. The door scraped across the floor when I opened it. The office was almost dark, but Joe was alone, standing behind his desk with his knuckles pressed into the wood. No sign of Rikki and Sabrina.

"Come in and close that, please."

I took one step forward. "Why is it so dark in here?"

Kennedy shut the door, trapping me between her and Joe. I could hear people mumbling in the changing room at the back of the office. Were Rikki and Sabrina in there? Would Joe really go back on his word? Grown-ups did that; they went back on their word. They did things without thinking how it could hurt a kid. A bolt of anger seared through me. Kennedy sensed it and grabbed my arms.

"Wait!"

Right then, the door to the dressing room burst open. Everything went from dark to light. From murky to clear. From rough to soft. From brown to pastels. A cluster of bodies moved out of the dressing room like they were bound together, determined to get through the door at the same time. Mom and Bryce and Jamie and Mr. McDaid were all stuck to one another, and they were all smiling. Mom held a round, slightly tilted, double-decker, aqua-blue birthday cake in her hands. The flames from a thousand yellow candles rose from the top, making her whole face glow.

"Happy birthday! Happy birthday!"

My knees felt weak as I listened to them sing that wonderful, awful birthday song in unison. My unison.

Our unison.

The unison of me and Mom and our new, chosen friends.

Wave after wave of raw sweetness swept over me. So many feelings bound together, I couldn't have sorted them if I'd wanted to. It was my thirteenth birthday, and in the end I was glad they all knew.

Bryce made hot chocolate in Styrofoam cups, and I sank a knife deep into the fluffy cake, grinning so wide my jaw actually ached more than the rest of my body.

"Your lip is banged up," Mom said.

Bryce laughed. "Yeah, you look like a boxer. Took a spill on your first canter, huh?"

I looked quickly to Joe, hoping and praying he hadn't told anyone the Rikki-and-Sabrina part.

"Rusty took the spill," he said. "Lizzie just happened to go with him."

Jamie chuckled. "Every time Kennedy fell off a pony when she was little, she told me—"

"—you're not a real rider until you've come off at least a hundred times," she finished.

"I think Kennedy really wanted to be a gymnast but was too tall, so she made up for that by vaulting from the back of every pony she rode," Jamie said.

"Not true." Kennedy shook her head and stuffed another piece of cake into her mouth. A bit of blue frosting dotted the end of her nose.

"I was there for almost all the falls," Joe said. "I think your dad might have a point."

"I object to your comment, sir," she said, grinning. "Bryce, how many times have you fallen off since you started riding?"

Bryce was perched on the edge of the desk with a cup of hot chocolate in his hands and a brown mustache on his upper lip.

"Too many to count," he said. "But the good news is, even with all our falls, Kennedy and I survived. So will Lizzie."

Mr. McDaid leaned toward Mom like they were in cahoots about something. "It's an initiation thing. A fall here and there just toughens you up. Little Lizzie will be fine."

Bryce flinched. He looked at his dad like he didn't want him to be part of our group. Mom smiled, but I could tell the whole idea of my falling made her nervous. Kennedy saw it, too, and changed the subject.

"Speaking of which," she said to me, "we have a gift."

She held out a small velvet box.

"For me?"

"Of course for you, unless there's someone else in here with a birthday we didn't sniff out!" Mr. McDaid said.

I rubbed my fingers over the fuzzy top and opened the lid. Inside was a tiny gold locket, no bigger than my thumbnail, shaped like a heart, and hanging from a delicate gold chain.

"Look inside," Mom said.

The locket popped right open. Inside was a miniature picture of Fire with his forelock falling over his eyes.

"Oh," I said. "Oh."

"I guess 'oh' means you like it?" Kennedy asked.

"I love it so much. I don't know what to say."

Mom lifted the hair from my neck and fastened the chain so the locket hung just above my heart. I went into the dressing room where they'd all been hiding and looked at my reflection in the mirror. My eyes were glistening, and my swollen lip was turning purple. But none of that mattered, because the girl staring back at me was happy.

TWENTY

I carried the last piece of cake home in a McDonald's bag left over from Joe's breakfast. Jamie was driving Mom back to work, and Mr. McDaid took Bryce to a doctor's appointment.

When I came up behind the cedar tree, a black-capped chickadee flitted away from the empty bird feeder, calling high-low notes from the snowy branch of a birch. *Feed-me, feed-me.* My pockets were empty. I'd forgotten to bring a handful of sweet-feed from Birchwood. Instead, I crumbled the last slice of cake into the base for the birds to share. Who would have fed the birds if we hadn't come to Good Hope?

Miss May stopped me in the hall, her face stern. "You have mail," she said, as if my having mail had been a terrible inconvenience to her. She jerked her head toward the table by the front door. "In the basket."

A manila envelope sat on top with *Elizabeth St. Clair* typed on the label. In the upper left corner was the name and address of Mom's lawyer in New Haven. I tore the envelope open and pulled out another one, robin's-egg blue, the size and shape of a birthday card. No return address but none needed. It was from Dad. I stalled for a second, holding the envelope over the trash can, then changed my mind and raced to my room.

Lizzie St. Clair.

He'd written my name in the funny half-script he used back when he would leave Mom and me notes on the fridge: kind of curly with big loops and long tails. Inside the bottom of the *z*'s he'd drawn happy faces, and the *i* in our last name was dotted with an open heart. I sat on the bed and traced each letter with my fingertip. Twelve months had gone by since everything had changed. An entire year of longing and fear and missing him, then anger. So much anger. Then nothing. What could he possibly say in a single birthday card that would give me back those twelve months? What could take away the pain of knowing he'd done a crime and then discarded Mom and me?

I slipped my thumb under the sealed edge and lifted the flap.

Dear, sweet Lizzie,

I hope you get this card. It's all I've got for right now, but you deserve so much more. I can't believe you are turning thirteen. A teenager. My Lizzie. I hope, too, that we can talk soon and I can explain. I know you must think I am a horrible, terrible person. I miss your hugs and your fuzzy blue slippers.

Happy birthday, my beautiful girl.

Love,

Dad

He didn't even know my fuzzy blue slippers were in a storage unit somewhere and I'd probably outgrown them by now. I read the card twice, three times, waiting to feel something. Anything. Relief. More anger. Regret.

Maybe a part of me was still hoping he would say he was innocent. Or that he was guilty but he was sorry. Maybe then the long overdue combustion of emotion simmering inside would ignite. Maybe then I wouldn't care who found out what he'd done. Maybe then I wouldn't care what he'd done, either.

But there was nothing.

I took off my coat, my hat, and my boots, and lay on Mom's bed, pressing the card to my heart, waiting for tears. Nothing came but sleep.

When I woke up, the heater puffed out air, and bright yellow fabric I hadn't noticed before swayed in front of the window. I rolled off the bed and stumbled across the room.

Yellow curtains—fresh, clean yellow, not the stained, off-white leftovers that were so old and bogged down with years of wear they didn't even flutter when we'd opened the window this summer. I touched the crisp fabric and rubbed it between my fingers. It was new, and very real. Mom had spent money on an unessential item for my birthday. It could only have been Mom. No one else knew this fabric was exactly the same as my bedroom curtains back home. Yellow-and-white plaid with tiny red birds.

I crawled to the top bunk, dug out my old poetry notebook, and started writing. Outside, in the gray light of a winter afternoon, a blue jay flew behind the cedar tree to get his cake.

TWENTY-ONE

The next Friday, the weekend before school started back up, Mr. McDaid picked up me and Bryce at Birchwood to drive us to the indoor polo match. To keep Good Hope a secret from them, Mom and I had concocted a plan where they would drop me off at O'Toole's pub afterward. Jamie already knew where we lived and why, and he could drive Mom and me home together.

"I'll show you everything," Bryce said in the car. "It's easier than anything you do at Birchwood, and it's fun. Plus, moola." He rubbed his fingers together.

We pulled up a dirt driveway to a red barn at least three

times as big as Birchwood and stopped next to a life-sized statue of a man jumping a horse over a fence.

"That guy used to ride here," Bryce said. "He was in the Olympics."

Mr. McDaid handed Bryce a crisp twenty-dollar bill. "Here's some money for hot chocolate for Lizzie. You two stay warm."

"That's a lot of hot chocolate," I said when Mr. McDaid left.

"Yeah, well, I'll buy some for you, but I'm keeping the rest of the money myself."

I shook off the unpleasant sense of envy and followed him inside a spacious building where steam from sweaty horses raised the temperature by at least fifteen degrees.

"We'll wait over there," Bryce said, pointing to a wall on the other side, right next to a solid double gate.

Horses pranced all around us, chomping on their bits, their tails bound up and wrapped tight so they looked like dogs who'd had their tails docked. The polo match hadn't started yet, but most of the horses were already sweaty. The riders buckled their helmets and spurs while sitting on horses so worked up, they couldn't keep all four feet on the ground at the same time. One by one, the players grabbed their mallets, then urged their horses forward and cantered off into the ring. Finally, the last one was in. A big double door closed, a loud buzzer sounded, and cheers went up in the stands.

"Whoa," I said. "A girl could get killed standing in the wrong place."

"There is truth in that," Bryce said. He held out the twenty-dollar bill. "They've just started the first chukka, so if you want a hot chocolate, now's the time to get it."

I could hear the horses' hooves pounding the earth inside the ring. The ball made a *thwack!* sound when a mallet connected with it and a *thud* every time it hit a wall. People cheered, the riders yelled, and the mallets kept swinging. A jolt of adrenaline rushed through my veins. I shook my head.

"I want to stay here and listen to them play."

Bryce leaned against the wall and grinned. "Uh-huh. Another one bites the dust."

"What does that mean?"

"Polo is addictive. Sounds like the bug might have already bitten you, and you haven't even seen a game yet."

I stood on my tiptoes to try and see over the top of the gate. Riders raced by on their horses, back and forth, back and forth, until suddenly a roar of cheers went up, a buzzer sounded again, and the gate to the ring burst open. Bryce grabbed my jacket sleeve and snatched me out of the path of hot horses streaming from the ring. A man on a tall gray gelding dismounted and handed Bryce his reins.

"Thanks, kid," he said.

Someone else held out the reins of a fresh horse. The man mounted swiftly, guzzled from a bottle of orange Gatorade, and was gone.

Bryce led the gray horse away from the crowd. I started to

follow him, but he turned and said sharply, "No, wait there for yours!"

"My what?"

"Your horse! Just stay. I'll be over here."

I pressed my body against the wall, out of the way of nervous horses and flying hooves. Sweaty riders dismounted, rehydrated, and mounted new horses, then spun around and spurred them into the ring. A woman trotted up on a bay that was nearly as tall as any Clydesdale I'd ever seen in a commercial. She jumped off and handed me the reins like she'd been expecting me to be there.

"Thanks," she said. "I'm only switching for one chukka, so don't go too far."

A man led over a smaller black mare. The mare's flanks already shined with sweat, and her eyes darted nervously.

"Hold on, Missy," the lady said. She had her left foot in the stirrup, but Missy kept spinning in circles and lunging toward the gate. The man grabbed her bridle and held her still for the two seconds it took the rider to leap into the saddle and take off. The gates closed again and another buzzer rang.

The bay horse beside me huffed and puffed and rubbed his mouth against my jacket, leaving a mark of white slobber on my sleeve.

"Hey, Lizzie!"

Bryce waved me over. I zigzagged through the crowd, bringing the bay along while dodging his giant hooves.

"Holy moly," I said. "That was crazy!"

"Yeah, you gotta move fast. Come on, let's walk. Did you loosen his girth?"

"No, I didn't know I was supposed to."

"Just like at Birchwood. Loosen his girth two holes, then right before the end of the next chukka, get him a drink, tighten it back up, and be ready by the gate for his rider."

"I thought you said we were walking polo ponies," I said, loosening the giant bay's girth. "I haven't seen one pony yet, and here I end up with this guy whose head is as big as a half bale of hay!"

"You won't see any ponies here. They're just called that because they have to be quick and agile, like a pony."

"What's a chukker?"

"Not chukker, duh. It's a chukk-*a*," he said, grinning. "It's a time frame like innings in baseball but about seven minutes instead of three outs. The whole game is six chukkas plus breaks in between."

We walked down an aisle that was twice as long as any at Birchwood. At the end, instead of spilling to an outdoor riding ring, the barn curved to the left for another stretch, then another, and we walked back up to the area outside the ring. After two trips around the barn, Bryce checked his watch and led me to a long metal water trough.

"Only let them drink to the count of ten," he said. "No more than that."

Both horses dunked their noses into the water, and Bryce counted out loud.

". . . eight, nine, ten," he said.

We pulled them away with water still dribbling and tightened the girths. A minute later, the buzzer sounded again, the gate to the indoor ring flew open, and a whole new set of hot and sweaty horses rushed out. The lady on the black mare found me and jumped off.

"You give him a little drink?" she asked, taking the reins of the bay.

"Yes, until the count of ten, and his girth is tight."

"Good job. Thanks, kid."

She handed me Missy's reins and pulled a crumpled ten-dollar bill from her pocket.

"Lucky you. I forgot to get fives today. There you go. Leg up?"

She faced the side of the bay horse and bent her knee. I grabbed it with my free hand, helped her into the saddle, and the bay horse whirled around.

"Missy's cooler is hanging on the wall," she called over her shoulder. "The red one, gold tie in the front, only one like it. Thanks!"

Missy's breath came much harder than the bay's had. Sweat laced her eyelashes. I wiped them dry with my sleeve and loosened her girth two holes, then laid the red flannel sheet over her back. "Good girl, Missy."

Bryce was waiting for me in the same place.

"You loosen the girth?"

"Of course."

He raised his hand for a high five.

For well over two hours, Bryce and I walked polo ponies used in two separate matches. We gave them water, loosened and tightened girths, and hoisted riders into saddles. Before we left, the lady who rode Missy told me her name was Kate.

"I've never seen you here before, but I hope you'll come back. You're responsible. We don't always get responsible kids to hot-walk," she said. "What's your name?"

"Lizzie."

She put her hand out. "Nice to meet you, Lizzie. And welcome to the polo family."

Inside me, everything glowed as bright and warm as the candles on my birthday cake.

Bryce and I stood outside under new falling snow after everything was over, waiting for Mr. McDaid. Bryce pulled wads of money from his pocket and counted.

"How much did you make?" I asked.

"Seventy-five. You?"

"Eighty."

He shoved me playfully. "Hey, no fair. Here I bring you to help and you make more money than me. How does that work out?"

I laughed, and he laughed and bumped my shoulder with his. My toes were frozen inside my paddock boots, my feet throbbed and my legs ached, my nose was red from the cold, my shirt was soaked in sweat underneath my jacket, and I hadn't gotten my cup of hot chocolate. But that was okay, because instead I was eighty dollars closer to buying Fire.

That night, I started a whole new page to keep track of my growing savings account.

TO BUY FIRE

$1,000

–245 (carried over)

= $755

–80

= $675 to go

In only two months I'd earned almost thirty-three percent of what I needed. There were seven more weeks of indoor polo. Seven times eighty would give me another five hundred and sixty dollars. That would be the beginning of March. If Angela kept paying me and the polo money kept coming in, and no one else bought Fire first, I could make it.

That was too many *what if*s. What if I didn't make eighty dollars every time? What if I was sick on a Friday and couldn't go? What if Angela lost her job? Or Mom found out and said I had to give the money back? I had to figure out another way to make more money. I lay on my bunk and massaged my stomach, trying to work the knots out. There had to be something I wasn't thinking of where I could earn more money faster.

TWENTY-TWO

I'd like to sell these, please."

A man with a bald spot on the very top of his head was crawling around on the thrift store floor, picking up assorted shoes and nylon footies someone had left scattered. He tossed each into a pile, then looked up at me, his face red, like he was annoyed I'd disturbed him. When he saw the four stuffed animals in my arms, everything about him softened.

"Awwww, what have we here?"

He stood up and wiped dust from his pant legs, then took the palomino pony from my arms.

"I'd like to sell these," I repeated. "Do you know how much I can get?"

"These are adorable. My own kid would love this pony. Well, she would have in days gone by. You've outgrown them, huh?"

I nodded. I didn't trust myself to say yes out loud.

He examined the palomino pony from forelock to tail, then took the golden retriever and checked the seam where Mom had sewn his head together after the ear got chewed up by the vacuum cleaner.

"Well, that makes for an interesting look," he said, smiling. "Let's go see what the others sell for. Stuffed animals are always popular here."

I followed him to the far wall where a basket of ragtag puppies and kittens and even a goldfish sat beneath some shelves. He fingered the price tags of a few.

"We're selling these guys for eight dollars each," he said. "Fifty percent of that goes to the consignor. That's you, a consignor."

He said *consignor* really slow, like maybe he thought I was stupid.

"So four dollars each?"

"If they sell; not everything sells. We keep things for two months. If they don't sell, you come back and pick them up."

Sixteen dollars. I held them a little tighter. The man folded his hands in front of himself and looked thoughtful.

"Tell you what," he said. "These are nicer than the others. Even with the stain and the missing ear, I could probably sell yours for twelve bucks each. That would give you six dollars for each one that sold. If they sell. Not everything sells."

I looked at the golden retriever and remembered that day when I had to pick what I brought with me to Good Hope and what got left behind.

"So that would be twenty-four dollars. If they sell," he repeated again.

The koala bear's fur was the softest of all four, but the pony and the golden retriever had always been my favorites.

Twenty-four dollars.

Fire.

"Okay," I said, handing them over. "I'll do it."

The man had me fill out a Consignor's Agreement while he arranged the animals in the basket. He propped the golden retriever's head over the side of the wicker, just like I had it at home.

"We don't call when something sells, but we keep a log and you can check back whenever you want. We pay out the first and fifteenth of each month. So even if one sells today or tomorrow, you wouldn't get paid until the fifteenth."

"Thank you."

"Well, good, then," he said.

I looked past him to the basket, said a silent goodbye, and fled down the stairs.

That night I wrote in a new extra section in my savings notebook, showing how much I might get: *Possible money from stuffed animals $24.*

The next day—the last day before school started again—I went back to the thrift store. The same man was there.

"Oh, hello. More stuffed animals?"

I shook my head. "I have some clothes that don't fit anymore. My mom said to bring them."

Liar.

I handed over two pairs of jeans, still in near-perfect condition. The man looked at the labels, then glanced at me suspiciously.

"And your mom does know you're selling these?"

I nodded, my face burning. I tried not to look in the direction of the basket, but I couldn't help it. All four animals were still there.

"Hmm, okay. Well, these are Gucci jeans, and they look almost new. I can't price them as high as they should be priced because we don't have that kind of clientele, but I can put them out at fifty dollars and see what we get for them."

"How much are they new?"

"New? In the city? Over two hundred bucks. For a silly pair of jeans. My kid would kill for these. So are you good with that?"

I could get fifty dollars altogether if both pairs sold.

"Yes, that's fine," I said.

We did the same thing as the day before, but this time I didn't need to say goodbye. I couldn't have cared any less about those jeans.

Possible money from Gucci jeans $50.

At school the next day, all I could think about was the money I was hoping to make. Still, I waited for two days to pass before I went back, hoping the man wouldn't remember me. But he wasn't even there. It was a lady instead, with gray hair in tight curls, thick ankles, and heavy, scuffed-up shoes. She looked up from her newspaper when she saw me climb the stairs lugging my weighted-down backpack.

I pulled out of the pack the big book of horse photos Dad had given me and laid it on the counter. "I'd like to sell this."

"Oh, my. This is a horse-girl's dream book," she said. "My granddaughter would love this."

She licked her fingertip and scanned through page after page of the full-color horse photos I'd drooled over and studied countless times.

"Do you know how much I could get for it?"

She closed the book and pushed it toward me on the counter. "We are on top of the library. We don't sell books here. I'm sorry."

"Oh, right. I hadn't thought about that."

I heaved the book into my backpack and turned to the stairs, forcing my eyes not to look in the direction of the stuffed-animal basket.

"Young lady," the woman said. "Wait one second."

She came out from behind the counter and handed me a business card.

"If you still want to part with it, there is a homeless shelter for families right around the corner, just off Brook Drive. It's called Good Hope. I'm sure there are children there who would absolutely love that book."

I stared at the card with Miss May's name on the front and a picture of happy children playing under the oak trees in the front yard.

"Thank you," I said. "I'll do that."

I sprinted down the stairs, waving at Linda as I passed her desk on the way out. She watched me fly by with a worried expression on her face.

"See you Saturday!" I said.

"Okay!" She gave me a thumbs-up. "See you then!"

TWENTY-THREE

Ms. Fitzgerald was absent the first few weeks of January because of a death in her family. The substitute teacher was fine, but she didn't know anything about my poem and it being printed in the high school newspaper. I was antsy to get my copy and bring it home for Mom. I didn't have to wait too long, though, because on the second Thursday that Ms. Fitzgerald was gone, Jasmine brought a copy to school with her. As soon as I got settled at my desk for history class, all four girls descended on me.

"My brother brought this home from the high school yesterday," Jasmine said. "Your poem's in it."

She had the newspaper folded back so "Behind Birchwood" was typed across the top.

"It's a good poem, Lizzie," Jade said.

Rikki nodded in agreement. "Congrats on getting it published."

"Thanks."

Sabrina said, "Well, even with the poem being published and all, what we really wanted to tell you is that you shouldn't go into those woods back there."

"Yeah, no one goes back there." Jade raised her eyebrows. "Ever."

It was obvious from the way Jasmine was looking at me that she'd put two and two together and realized I was the kid sitting on the stone wall last summer, spying on their riding lesson. She knew that this poem came from my firsthand observations. She didn't look mad; instead she looked a little sad, like she pitied me. I didn't want pity.

"Why shouldn't I go back there?"

They closed in around my desk.

Rikki lowered her voice. "There's a homeless shelter back there."

The other three nodded solemnly. I trained my eyes on the grooves someone had dug in the top of my desk and ran my finger over the tiny gutter.

"I mean, you just never know what kind of people could be lurking around in those woods," Jade said.

Sabrina flipped a braid over her shoulder. “Yeah, my dad says homeless people will say anything to try to get money from you.”

Jasmine hadn’t taken her eyes off me and looked genuinely worried. “Really, girl, be careful.”

No words would come from my mouth. Nothing. So I smiled and nodded, like I was agreeing. Like I appreciated their warning and their description of the Homeless.

Of me.

Coach Redmond came into the room tossing a football in the air.

“Okay, class, let’s go, let’s go, let’s go!” He always talked like that, like he was on the sidelines of a football game trying to pump up his team. “Everyone into your seats. We’ve got drills to work on today!”

“We just thought you should know, that’s all,” said Sabrina quickly.

“Girls in the back of the room, whatever is distracting you, get over it!”

Jasmine patted my shoulder. “Be careful, Lizzie,” she said.

As they moved toward their desks, one of them said, “We warned her. That’s all we can do.”

I slumped down low in my seat and barely looked up when Bryce came in five minutes late. I was relieved that he didn’t try to catch my eye; I didn’t want him to see that I was in danger of crying.

* * *

The next weeks went by fast. I couldn't shake the ugly feeling that clung to me after I had nodded in agreement with Jasmine and her friends about homeless people being dangerous. Even though Leonard always looked like he hated being in the same room with me and even though I'd never played Monopoly with them again, none of the people at Good Hope were dangerous. I knew that. They were just like me and Mom. Something had happened that put them in a tough spot, and they were trying to get out.

I put my head down again and focused all my energy on keeping to myself and earning money. On Tuesdays and Thursdays, when the girls came for their lessons, I made sure I was occupied in a different part of the barn so we didn't have to make eye contact. And I also made sure to stay long after they left so they wouldn't see me walking myself home right through those woods.

One afternoon in the first week of February, I tallied up all the money hidden next to my mattress, then wrote the amount earned from each category on a new sheet of paper.

TO BUY FIRE

$1,000

<u>–245 (previous page)</u>

= $755

–300 (polo)

= $455

–24 (stuffed animals)

= $431

–28 (Angela)

=$403

–25 (Gucci jeans—1 pair)

= $378 to go

There was six hundred and twenty-two dollars. That total assumed I'd win the poetry contest, which was two weeks away. Even with that, it still wouldn't be enough. I stared at the numbers for a long time. Fire's training was going well. He was getting stronger—so he'd be more appealing to potential buyers. Six hundred and twenty-two dollars felt as far from one thousand dollars as the sun was from the moon. It could take me a year to earn the remaining three hundred and seventy-eight if I didn't hustle.

When I got to Birchwood later and went to sign in for my working student duties, a couple of younger riding students, Becky and Melissa, were gossiping in the office.

"Mike always looks like he's in a bad mood, anyway," Becky said.

She was only ten, but her whole family owned horses and fox hunted. She'd been around Joe and Mike since she was born. Melissa was nine but had started riding at Birchwood in the Tiny Tykes class for five- and six-year-olds. They were good kids, but I was painfully aware that even though they were younger than me, they knew much more about horses and Birchwood than I did.

"Joe didn't look very happy about him showing up out of the blue, either," Melissa said.

"Especially when Mike told him, 'Go get Fire!'" Becky flung her arm and scowled like she was imitating Mike.

"What are you talking about?" I said.

"Mike showed up right after we got here and told Joe he had to bring Fire and show him what he'd learned," Becky said.

"I think he might have found a buyer," Melissa said.

I dropped the pen and slammed the clipboard onto the desk. "What?"

My voice screeched. Both girls looked startled, but I didn't wait to explain. I sprinted from the office and broke the no-running-in-the-barn rule all the way to Fire's stall. Luis stood in the otherwise empty stall, methodically tossing clumps of soiled shavings through the air into a wheelbarrow parked just outside the door.

"Where's Fire?" I asked.

"En el pequeño anillo," he said, pointing to the small private ring where Bryce had his dressage lessons.

When I got there, Joe was trotting Fire in figure eights on a loose rein. He pushed him into a canter, crossed the diagonal line, trotted a few steps, and changed leads. Fire was perfect. I watched from outside the gate until Joe brought Fire to a walk and let the reins slip through his hands.

"He's looking better," Mike said gruffly. "But I want him ready to sell by the end of this month. Show or no show. He's been eating up the profits since last fall."

The back of my knees felt like someone had swung a baseball bat into them. The end of the month. Less than four weeks. That was all the time I had left.

"Get it done." Mike turned to leave and nodded at me as he passed.

Joe jumped off Fire. "Hey, Lizzie, perfect timing. Wanna cool him out for me?"

I stepped into the ring, checking to be sure Mike was already out of hearing range. "I heard what he said."

Joe took his helmet off and ran his fingers through damp hair. "I'm sorry. But you've always known this was the plan."

"I didn't think it would be so soon."

"Mike owns this place," Joe said sadly. "At the end of the day, what he says goes."

"But, Joe, I'm saving money—"

I wanted to say I was only a few hundred dollars shy, but he cut me off.

"Lizzie, I wish I could hand him over to you and never charge you a penny for his board. But that's not why I bought him, and that's definitely not what Mike expects. Fire is going to make a nice little show pony for someone at another stable."

"Maybe he doesn't want to be a show pony at another stable."

"You're right, maybe he doesn't. But we don't always get to pick where we live, do we?" He paused for a second, struggling to keep his face from showing just how bad he felt for me. "Wherever that is, though, wherever we end up, it usually works out and we're okay."

I took the reins and rubbed my chest, trying to massage away the pinched feeling in the middle. "I'll cool him out and put him away."

"I'm sorry, Lizzie," he said.

Everything inside me froze. I felt nothing as Fire and I walked around and around the ring. There had to be something I could do. Some way to speed up earning more money. A few minutes went by and a string of adult riders came in, leading their horses to the middle of the ring.

"Drill team practice in five minutes," one of them said to me. Meaning I had to clear out of the ring for them.

"Thank you."

I walked Fire toward the gate. Another rider rushed past me, leading a horse with only three polo wraps on his legs. He had bits of hay clinging to his uncombed tail and a manure mark on his white saddle pad.

"Sorry I'm so disheveled," she said to the riders already in the ring. "I'll have my tack clean and all four polos before the next practice. I promise."

When Fire was back in his stall, I wrapped my arms around his neck and whispered close to his ear, "Don't worry, Fire. I'm going to earn that money in time. I promise."

The next day I posted signs by every tack room on the whole farm.

TACK CLEANING SERVICE
FEBRUARY SPECIAL!
COMPLETE CLEAN, CONDITION, AND POLISH
SADDLES: $10
BRIDLES: $5
BRIDLES W/BIT CLEAN & POLISH $8
MARTINGALES: $3
SEE LIZZIE TO SCHEDULE

Forty-eight hours later, six horse owners had signed up. Six saddles and bridles equaled ninety more dollars! The lady who'd bought Tiger Lily at Christmas brought me four fuzzy saddle pads to wash and said she'd pay three dollars each. Another person whose horse lived across the driveway in the boarder barn came to find me. She had four pairs of dirty polo wraps in a bag.

"If you roll them correctly," she said, "I'll give you two dollars a pair."

I was closing in on the entire thousand, and except for Mr. McDaid's one hundred dollars, I'd earned every penny of it honestly and through hard work. That night, I ran the whole way home, my fingers itching to mark everything in my notebook.

I got to the door at the same time as Angela. She looked like she needed a long vacation.

"You okay?" I asked. "Do you need help with the girls tonight?"

She set her bag down inside the door and shook her head. "Thanks for the offer, but Faith was extra clingy this morning. I want to spend some one-on-one time with them tonight. Valentine's is next week, though, and I'm working an extra day at the florist on Sunday. Could you help me then?"

"The whole day?"

"If possible. Lots of deliveries, so I should be able to share lots of tips with you."

"I can do it."

"Super! Rest up. That's a long day by yourself with three kids. Heck, that's a long day for me with three kids!"

"I need the money," I said. "Badly."

Angela took off the hat Mom had crocheted for her and tucked it under her arm. "Are you okay? You're not in some kind of trouble, are you?"

"No, nothing like that. I'm saving money, and I need to save more, faster."

"Ah," she said. "To help your mom? That's awesome, Lizzie."

Leonard came in and banged the door shut behind us,

stomping his feet on the mat. "You two plot to take over the world?"

Angela laughed. "No, we're talking about saving money."

Leonard's black eyes narrowed at me. "Yes, for the horse."

I reached down to pretend to tie my boot laces so Angela wouldn't see the truth on my face. Leonard's boot was a hand's width away from mine. I resisted the urge to reach out and punch it.

"Now where would you get a silly idea like that?" Angela said. "A horse? Do you forget we live in a homeless shelter?"

Leonard brushed past. "Yes, I remember bezdomnyy, but maybe I'm the only one."

I'd never really thought much about miracles, about whether they were real or just happy coincidences. But the very next day, more work for more money was plunked into my lap without my even asking. Joe came into the office right after I got to Birchwood and sat down in his chair.

"Just the person I needed to see," he said. "Wanna earn some money?"

I held the pen over the sign-in sheet and felt a jolt of relief. "Heck yeah. Doing what?"

"We're going to the big winter show this weekend in Simsbury, and I suddenly don't have a groom. Right now it's just me and Kennedy, but we'll be coaching."

"What happened to the person who was supposed to go?"

"Janet. Her grandma passed away. She's going out of town."

I'd heard Janet talk about working at the show in Simsbury. It was at one of the fanciest barns in the whole state. She'd been really excited.

"Does that mean I'd have to come Friday night to help get ready, too?"

"It does, so you'd have to skip the polo match, but you'd make a lot more money helping us. We've got fifteen kids going, and each of their parents contribute and tip the groom. You could make a hundred fifty, hundred sixty bucks for Friday night and Saturday day."

"Yikes! For real?"

"For real."

I did some mental math. If I got that much at the horse show, I'd only need another two hundred and twenty-eight dollars, and once I got paid for the tack I was cleaning I'd be even closer to the full thousand!

"Yeah, I'll do it," I said. "I'll let Bryce know I can't go with him."

"Great! Friday night we'll bathe and braid the horses and have pizza in the clubhouse, then we leave at five thirty Saturday morning. Tell your mom I can take you home Friday night and I'll pick you up at four forty-five on Saturday. She can call me if she has any questions. Oh, and no need to tell Bryce. He's one of the fifteen."

TWENTY-FOUR

Bryce was absent from school on Friday, and he was a no-show at Birchwood that night, too. The other fourteen riders flooded the barns like a school of starving fish. Trying to put a saddle away meant stepping over a whole slew of people sitting on the floor in the tack room. They were rubbing sponges wet with glycerin soap in circles on saddles, polishing silver bits with toothpaste, smearing shiny black polish over their tall leather boots, and talking about the show the next day. They waited impatiently in line to use the wash stalls to bathe their horses and called for Kennedy every time something happened they considered tragic.

"Kennedy, the edge of this strap on his girth is frayed. I can't use it!"

"Kennedy, Piglet won't pick up his hooves for me to clean them."

"Kennedy, I can't find Bluebell's left stirrup!"

Kennedy ran from group to group all evening, fixing problems and rolling her eyes every time she passed me.

Outside Joe's office, a bunch of parents had gathered in a group, waiting their turn to sign permissions slips and pay the show fees.

"Coldest day in twenty years," someone said. "And we get to take our kids to a horse show."

"Ha! Amanda will wait all year for the chance to stay out in the freezing weather at this show but says it's too cold to get out of bed on a school day."

"Wendy gets up Saturday mornings at six o'clock to get here and clean horse you-know-what all day, but her room is such a mess you can't see the floor."

"Excuse me," I said politely, trying to squeeze past them with my wheelbarrow full of horse show supplies. My breath made a cloud in front of me in the frigid air. Two people moved aside, but no one offered to help me trudge across the frozen tundra to the trailer.

"The way I figure," a dad said, "this will keep her occupied until past her initial boy-crush phase. Maybe she'll have more sense than other girls about all that."

I wrangled the wheelbarrow over the bumpy ground and unloaded grain, lead ropes, buckets, and blankets into the tack room of the trailer. By the time the pizza came, I'd hauled bags of shavings, bales of hay, water buckets, and extra halters and saddle pads across the ice in the dark and loaded them by myself. My arms and back ached. Droplets of sweat crystalized on my forehead before I could wipe them off. I was hanging the last of the bridles on the hooks when Joe stuck his head in.

"Hey, kiddo, pizza's here. Come on in. You've earned your keep for the night."

He pushed the empty wheelbarrow back to the barn for me. "Everything okay? You hanging in there?"

"Yeah," I said. "Just cold."

"Single digits tonight. Bring ChapStick tomorrow and extra clothes in case you get wet."

"Where's Bryce?"

Joe leaned the wheelbarrow against the wall and rolled the door closed. The barn was empty now. Braided horses munched on hay in their stalls, and the kids had already gone to the clubhouse to eat pizza.

"He didn't tell you?"

"Tell me what?"

"I couldn't let him come. He hasn't taken the show team lessons. It's part of his dad's requirement."

"But he takes lessons with Kennedy."

"Not the same. He knows the deal. Michael said he could have the dressage lessons so long as he learned equitation, too."

"But he doesn't like equitation; he likes dressage."

Joe shook his head. "Not my rule, Lizzie. His dad is in charge of all that."

"Is he in trouble?"

"With me? No. With Michael? Maybe. He wasn't too happy when I called to tell him why Bryce couldn't go."

My stomach felt like someone had planted a heel right in the center of it.

It was after eleven o'clock before I crawled into bed. I tossed and turned and tried to sleep but finally got up, took Mom's phone into the bathroom, and sent Bryce a text.

Joe said you can't go to show hope ur ok Mom's phone don't reply.

I deleted the text and set the phone back on the windowsill. It was three thirty. I had to be up in less than an hour.

Eight horses and ponies were loaded into two trailers by 5:35 on the dot. We pulled out of the driveway in the dark only ten minutes later than Joe had planned.

"Not bad timing," Kennedy said, sipping a cup of coffee and expertly maneuvering the trailer up the icy driveway. "Not bad at all."

The ride to the show was going to be the last bit of quiet for the day. Kennedy kept her eyes on the road, and I scribbled words in a fresh spiral notebook. Working as a groom wasn't exactly how I had imagined my first horse show would go, but no matter how I got there, or that I'd be working instead of riding, it was my first. The day deserved at least the start of a poem to celebrate.

An hour later, our trailers were parked in a frozen field at the show grounds. Joe and I tacked up the horses while Kennedy went to register the riders for their classes.

"Keep your eye on Bluebell," Joe said before the start. The pony laid her ears back when he tightened the girth and swung her head around. Joe's elbow met her teeth before they could sink into his arm. "Bluebell is a perfect example of my 'ponies are reincarnated ax murderers' theory. Stay ringside when she's in a class, just in case."

"What will she do?"

"Hopefully nothing, but if she decides she's done for the day, she'll take the bit in her teeth and make a run for the gate."

A little red-haired girl called Georgia was Bluebell's first victim. During a Walk-Trot class, Bluebell took off from the far side of the ring and ran diagonally through the middle toward the exit. Georgia clung to the pommel of the saddle and screamed the whole way, until the pony skidded to a halt at the gate. Georgia leaned forward and threw up. Her dad grabbed her, and I whisked the pony away to clean her up before the next class. That was my job. Cleaning throw-up out of wicked ponies' manes.

Apparently, I was also the official Birchwood cell phone photographer. I took dozens of pictures of happy riders proudly holding up the colorful ribbons they'd won, surrounded by moms and dads and brothers and sisters. Even little Georgia smiled after her embarrassing finale.

"Thanks a lot, Lizzie," her dad said when I handed him back his phone. "Come find us after you show and we'll take your picture. That way your mom and dad can be in it, too."

I didn't know what to say, so I mumbled, "Thanks," and steered Bluebell toward a quiet spot away from the crowds. We both needed a little alone time to regroup. A few minutes later, Joe rushed over and felt Bluebell's chest.

"She's cool enough; get her a drink of water," he said. "She's got another class in fifteen minutes. God save the kid who rides her next."

He hurried off, and I led Bluebell to the closest trough. A girl brought a tall bay pony with crooked braids up beside us.

"Do you mind if we share?"

"Oh, sure."

Both ponies dunked their muzzles in the water and drank.

"I always like coming to this show because they have these troughs everywhere," the girl said. "Our trailer is parked on the far side of the field. I'd be out in the freezing cold hauling water buckets all day without this."

"Yeah," I said, pretending I already knew this. "Me too."

"I'm Ashley. We're from Riding Ridge in Poughkeepsie."

"Wow, that's far," I said.

"Yeah, but this is the best show in winter, and they give good prizes. Have you seen the trophies?"

"Yeah. Crazy."

"You're from Birchwood?"

"Oh, sorry. I'm Lizzie."

"I saw your jacket. Nice place. Are you showing today?"

"No," I said, shaking my head. "Not this time."

Ashley nodded sympathetically. "We take turns at being a groom, too, so the newer riders have a chance to ride."

I let her assume that's why I wasn't showing. It sounded more noble than the truth, which was that no one asked me if I wanted to show. I was already cantering and going over small jumps. Seems like I could have at least qualified for a Walk-Trot class.

A big fat lie spilled from my mouth. "I outgrew my show coat," I said. "Haven't gotten a new one yet."

"You're lucky," Ashley said. "My older sister showed all over the East Coast before she went to college, so my parents make me wear her hand-me-downs."

"What's your pony's name?" I asked.

"Benjamin Bunny. Ben for short."

"Cute."

"What about yours?"

"Bluebell, for the one blue eye, but she's a reincarnated ax murderer, if you know what I mean," I said.

Ashley laughed, and I laughed, and for a second I felt like I wasn't pretending to fit in. But then, Ben lifted his face from the trough. A thick stream of yellow mucus ran from his nose, right into the water. My stomach lurched, and I yanked Bluebell's lead rope to pull her head away.

"Looks like Ben needs a tissue," Ashley said. "Well, see ya. Good luck to your riders today. We'll be in Vermont this summer, so if you guys go, come find me and we can hang out."

"Sure," I said, although I had no idea where in Vermont she would be, and I already knew I wouldn't be there. too.

TWENTY-FIVE

A little after one o'clock, Kennedy told me to take a break. "Hey, time to eat lunch. Come with me."

Lunch. I hadn't even thought to bring anything to eat. My stomach growled.

"You look like a deer in headlights. Don't worry: Joe always buys for us on show days. This place has the best Frito pies ever. I'm starving."

"What's a Frito pie?"

"You'll see. Come on."

We sat together in a heated clubhouse, each with a bowl of Fritos layered with a mound of chili, shredded cheddar cheese, and a big dollop of sour cream on top. A little pile of spicy jalapeños on the side of Kennedy's plate burned my nose.

"So, the horse show. What do you think so far?" she asked.

My mouth was full of chili and cheese. I nodded and gave her a thumbs-up.

"Man, I remember my first show. Holy smokes, it was culture shock." She pointed her spoon at me. "Believe it or not, there was a time in my life when I was shy. And quiet. I bet that surprises you. Anyway, my first show was a winter one, like this, only I didn't have warm-enough clothes. At least you have warm clothes. Did you bring ChapStick?"

"Yup."

"Good. Your lips are already getting raw. It's the wind with the cold air. Use it when we're finished. Anyway, I got frostbite. See?"

She held out her left hand and showed me the tips of her fingers. The skin on two of them was slightly darker than the others and wrinkled.

"Yikes! How'd that happen?"

"Horse show, no mittens, ten degrees. I had water bucket duty. That's why we don't make anyone go back to the trailer for water at winter shows anymore and why we don't let anyone be a groom until they're at least twelve. I was really little."

"Why didn't you wear mittens?"

"They fell in the water. Only pair I had."

"Was your mom mad?"

She shook her head, and her eyes clouded. "My mom was actively dying from cancer at the time. I don't even think she knew."

"Oh, I'm really sorry."

"It's okay. It happens."

"What about your dad?"

"My dad? If he'd been around, he probably would have used mitten money to buy whiskey."

"What?"

She looked at the shock on my face and shook her head. "Oh, I mean my biological father. Jamie adopted me after my mom died."

"Where's your real dad?"

"Jamie *is* my real dad. If you mean my biological father, I have no idea. Jail, maybe? He signed me over and disappeared as soon as he got my mom's life insurance check."

"What does that mean, 'signed you over'?"

"It means he discarded me. Guess he wanted to keep all that insurance money to himself." She spooned a big mound of jalapeños onto her chili and smiled at me before scooping it into her mouth. "Yum."

"Doesn't it bother you that he did that?"

"Life is full of challenges and opportunities, Lizzie. Sometimes they come in the same package. I mean, think about it. I got Jamie out of the deal. All my biological father got was money."

For the rest of the day, I couldn't stop thinking about Kennedy's words. On the drive home, she and I both were quiet, until I saw the barn lights of Birchwood shining like a beacon at the end of the long road.

"Can I ask you a question?"

"Shoot."

"How did Jamie adopt you? I mean, how'd you know him?"

She turned the radio off. "From the fire. He used to be a social worker before he started the pub."

"What fire?"

"The one at Good Hope, when Mom and I lived there."

"You lived at Good Hope?"

"Of course I did. You knew that. I told you."

"No, I'm pretty sure I'd remember that if you ever told me."

"Well, anyway, I did, for about six months. That's how I found Birchwood. I actually made that path you walk through those woods. Then there was the fire. Jamie came to see me in the hospital, and when I got out, I was going into foster care because my mom was at the very end. That's when he decided to be my dad."

"So, you and your mom lived there because you were homeless?"

She smiled, her eyes staring straight ahead. "Yup."

"Why?"

She snorted. "Why does anybody become homeless? Why do you live there?"

I turned my face to the window. I still wasn't ready to talk about what my dad had done.

"Well, then. Let me ask you a different question. Why does it surprise you that I lived there?" she asked.

"I don't know. I mean, you're so normal."

She glanced sideways. "What exactly does normal mean to you?"

"Like, you go to college, and you ride, and have a job, and you're going to be a photographer."

"Well, you ride. You'll go to college and have a job, too. And one of these days you'll wake up and realize you're living a new kind of normal, and it really isn't all that bad. I promise."

She flipped on the blinker to turn into the Birchwood driveway.

"I'm not so sure how much I trust promises," I said.

"Probably with good reason," she said. "But someday you'll understand which promises are trustworthy and which ones are empty."

"How old were you when you figured it out?"

She shrugged. "Not sure I know all the time even now. But have some faith in yourself. You're really doing A-OK."

I made one hundred and seventy dollars that day. It would have been less, but just before I left for home, Rikki surprised me.

"My grandma told me to give this to you," she said.

She held out a ten-dollar bill, twisting her mouth to the

side. We were standing outside under the floodlights on the icy driveway. Almost everyone else had gone home. A light snow started to fall, and a single flake dampened the end of Alexander Hamilton's nose. I looked back at Rikki's car, an ancient hippie van with flowers painted on the sides, where her grandmother was waiting with Rikki's dad.

The grandmother knew I needed money because she was the lady from the thrift store. The bald man, it turned out, was Rikki's dad. I pulled the hood of my jacket closer around my face.

"She already paid me," I said.

"I know. This is extra." She took my hand and closed my fingers around the bill. "You earned this, Lizzie. You worked hard today. See you Monday at school."

It was true. I'd worked hard for that money. Holding that extra ten dollars in my hand made something swell in me that felt good, and right. I was proud of my work and what I had honestly earned. If only Dad could have been satisfied with the same.

"See you Monday," I said.

Mom and Mrs. Ivanov were crocheting in the common room when I got home. I waved and made a mad dash past them to our room, in desperate need of a hot shower. Along with other unsavory aromas, I could still smell Georgia's throw-up on me. I stood under the stream and prayed there was enough hot water to get me through an entire shower. Once I was

Ivory-soap clean and in my pajamas, I climbed the ladder to my bunk, eager to pull up the covers and daydream about the horse show, and Kennedy, and my new semi-friendly feelings about Rikki. So many things were different after just one day.

The blue envelope with Dad's card was propped against my pillow. I hadn't thought of it once since my birthday. Laying my head back, I held the envelope up and studied the way he'd written my name on the front. When it had first arrived, his funny half-script had taken me back to our life before, and I'd felt sorry for myself. But now, looking at how carefully he'd written my name, I just felt sorry for *him*. And maybe a tiny bit nostalgic for the girl who'd once thought he was absolutely everything.

Mom came in a little later and tucked her crochet work into the basket sitting on the makeshift desk we'd put together with two boxes and a piece of particleboard left over from a project at her office.

"Mom?"

"Hi, sweetie. I wasn't sure if you were awake. How was the horse show?"

I turned on one elbow and looked at her from my bunk. "It was fun. I mean, it was a lot of work. My feet are killing me. But it was really good. My lips are chapped. Kennedy made me put ChapStick all over them, but they're really raw."

She stood on tiptoe to see and smiled. "Good for Kennedy. I like her."

“Me too.”

She got busy changing into her pajamas. Still nothing about the card.

“Mom?”

“Hmmm?”

“Did you read Dad’s card?”

“No. I found it under my bed this morning and left it for you.”

“It must have fallen under there. I forgot about it. I thought maybe he’d send money.”

“No money?”

“Of course not.”

“I’m sorry.”

“I didn’t expect it, really. Do you know when his trial is going to happen?”

“No, I don’t, but it doesn’t have an impact on us anyway.”

“I just want everything to be over.”

“I understand.”

“Do you think he misses us?”

“I would hope so, but he made his choice, Lizzie.”

“I know.”

She reached her hand over the top of my bunk and squeezed my arm. “We’re okay. You know that, right?”

“Yeah, I do. We’re making a new kind of normal.”

She smiled. “Yes, a new kind of normal. I like that.”

* * *

On Sunday evening, Mom rubbed menthol lotion into my sore shoulders.

"Ouch! What was I thinking?" I groaned.

"Maybe that you wanted to step up and help Angela?"

A tiny ping of guilt rose in me. Mom still didn't know I was getting paid for helping.

"Between the horse show yesterday and the girls all day today, I feel like I was run over by a truck. I don't even know if I can climb up to my bed."

"Oh, the drama."

"Easy for you to say: you've been crocheting all weekend."

"I did Saturday chores for both of us, remember, so you could go to the show. Nothing wrong with hard work. Hard work makes things happen for you."

"Yeah, well, this hard work is making me go right to bed. Good night."

Later, when Mom flipped on her reading light, I unfolded the money Angela paid me and counted. Twenty-three ones, four five-dollar bills, and one ten. Fifty-three dollars for the day with the girls. Fifty-three dollars closer to buying Fire. I added the money to the columns in my notebook and crossed off another day on the calendar I'd taped inside the cover. Eighteen days left to earn the rest of the money. I was going to make it. I just had to have a little faith in myself.

TWENTY-SIX

Bryce was grounded from everything except the barn, and he wasn't allowed lessons with Kennedy for a month.

"I don't know how much more I can take. He's such a jerk."

We were in the tack room after my working student duties were done on Wednesday, cleaning tack for more riders who had read my sign. The room smelled like glycerin soap and pony sweat.

"You don't think your mom can talk to him?"

He shot me a steely look and dipped his sponge into a

bucket of clean water. "I'm almost done with this saddle. How many more?"

"Two. Bridles are done and the saddle pads and polos are in the dryer."

"This was a smart idea. You saving for Fire?"

I'd never said anything to anyone, ever, about saving money for Fire. But that's how Bryce and I were. We knew each other.

"Yeah. I'm almost there."

"Cool. How much more do you need?"

"After I get paid for these, less than one hundred dollars. Joe told Mike he could get a thousand for Fire before he was a seasoned show pony. I'll be so close to a thousand."

"Wow. That's impressive, Lizzie."

"Yeah." I let his compliment sink in. "It is, isn't it?"

At lunch a couple of days later, I unwrapped the tuna sandwich Bryce brought for me, peeled off the crust, and tucked it into my pocket for the bird feeder.

"Does your dad ever ask why you bring all this extra food and still buy school lunch, too?" I asked. "Maybe he thinks you're trying to beef up. That ought to make him happy, right?"

Bryce had been melancholy all day, walking around with his head down and barely talking. He dragged a cold french fry through a mound of ketchup, then swirled it in circles and figure eights and serpentines until that poor slice of potato was a soggy red mess.

"I think I'm going home," he said.

I picked celery out of the tuna salad. "You sick?"

"No, I mean *home*-home. To Wyoming."

"What?"

He pushed the plate of fries away. "I can't do it. I can't stay with him."

"No, Bryce, you can't leave—" I stopped just shy of saying "me," but he knew. "You can't leave Tucker!"

"I'm not leaving Tucker. My mom is going to borrow the money to get him home."

"But why now? Is it because of the dressage?"

He shifted his head and pushed away the long bangs he often wore down over one side of his face, just enough for the fluorescent cafeteria lights to shine on a faint purple mark around his left eye.

"Where'd that come from?"

"Where do you think?"

"Bryce, no."

"Lizzie, yes."

He smashed his empty milk carton under his fist and tossed it like a basketball into the trash can in the corner.

"Not your dad," I said. "He couldn't—"

The first bell rang, and kids at the other tables got up and started shuffling toward the hallway. Neither Bryce nor I moved.

"Oh, yeah, he could. He did, and he will again if I stay."

"Have you told anyone? Like a teacher?"

He shook his head. "I told my mom, finally. I'd been hiding it from her, but every time I talked to her I felt guilty for letting her think I was okay. That's the way he makes me feel, like it's my fault."

The tardy bell rang. Bryce stayed in his chair, staring at the table with his head tilted again so his hair covered the bruise.

"We're late for class," I said gently. "You think you can go?"

He touched the bruise with his fingertips.

"Do you want me to get you a wet washcloth?"

He shook his head. "It's just going to take a few more days. It always does."

"He's done this before?"

"One too many times now." He looked up, his eyes half dead, half hopeful. "Want to go to the barn?"

"Now?"

"Yeah, now."

"You mean like skipping school?"

He pushed his chair back and shot up. "It's okay. Forget I said anything."

"No, wait," I said. "Come on, let's go."

He shouldered the backpack and let his bangs fall over the left side of his face again.

"Follow right behind me," he said. "Don't look at anyone. Eyes on the ground. Got it?"

"Got it."

Bryce knew a back way to get from our school to Birchwood. We walked up a long hill and through a field leading to the woods where my stone wall was almost hidden by snow.

"Wait here," Bryce said. He darted across the ring and peered into the barn, then waved for me to come. "All clear!"

I ran in behind him and followed him up the ladder to the hayloft. In the very back, behind stacks of hay and racks of saddles and assorted tack that needed to be repaired, Bryce had carved out a little cubby for himself. He unfolded an old horse blanket and laid it on the floor.

"Gotta have some kind of cushion, otherwise the hay pricks through your jeans."

"Do you come here a lot?"

"Eh," he said, shrugging.

We both sat on the blanket. Spanish music drifted up from the radio below.

"Can I use your cell to text my mom?" I asked.

"What are you going to tell her?"

"That I'm at the barn. If the school calls and says I'm missing, she'll freak out."

"Will she tell my dad?"

"Not a chance." I made an X over my heart. "Promise."

I tapped the buttons for her number.

ME: **It's me, Lizzie. This is Bryce's phone. I'm at barn, explain later. I'm fine. Please do NOT tell Mr. McDaid.**

A few minutes went by before she answered.

MOM: Is everything okay?

ME: I'm fine, don't tell Joe or anyone we're here.

MOM: What's going on? You're worrying me!

Bryce read the text. "Tell her there's a sick pony you were worried about."

ME: There's a sick pony. I'll explain later promise <3

MOM: Should I come?

ME: No! I'm fine.

MOM: K

ME: Can you call Miss May and tell her I'm going straight to Birchwood after school?

MOM: You're asking me to lie?

ME: Not a lie. I went to school, now I'm at Birchwood.

MOM: Too smart for your own britches but okay. <3

I clicked the phone off and leaned back against stacked bales of hay.

"Nice that your mom is like that," Bryce said.

"Yeah. I lucked out."

"What about your dad? What's he like?"

I picked at a piece of hay, then held it to my nose and inhaled the sweet aroma that never failed to make something warm and happy bloom in me.

"I used to think he was perfect. I guess in a way I thought he was the biggest piece of us, our family, like if he wasn't here, we wouldn't be us. But I was wrong."

"You wanna talk about it?"

Yes.

No.

Never.

Desperately.

Speak!

"He traded us in for a lady who could pay his bond so he didn't have to stay in jail until his trial. Mom couldn't pay to get him out because they froze all our money because he embezzled from his company."

"Ouch."

"Yeah. He got out before we moved here, and I didn't even know it. He's been out this whole time, living with some lady with money, and he's never even told me he's sorry. He's never even admitted what he did was wrong and hurt us, even after we had to move—"

I shut the words off. Bryce didn't ask what I meant. Maybe he already knew Mom and I lived in a homeless shelter. But after saying everything about Dad out loud for the first time, suddenly the part about living at Good Hope didn't seem to matter as much. It wasn't what I'd been hiding all along.

"Parents trick you," Bryce said. "I thought my dad changed after he and Mom got divorced. I thought it hurt him enough that he would be nicer, but that only lasted long enough to get me and Tucker here. He's never going to change. Since I've been here, he's only gotten worse."

"What did your mom say when you told her?"

"She cried. I didn't tell her for a long time, but I can't live here with him."

I wanted desperately to say something brilliant that would comfort him, something that would make him feel the tiniest bit better, but I had nothing. There just wasn't the right combination of words to take away what had happened. Instead, I slipped my hand into his and we sat in silence, listening to the Spanish ballads playing below.

TWENTY-SEVEN

Neither of us heard Joe climb the ladder until he had come around to the back and found us. I jerked my hand away from Bryce's.

"Hey, guys, what's going on here?"

"We're skipping school," Bryce said.

"I gathered that, but why? What's up?"

"My mom knows," I said. "I can show you the text. I told her there was a sick pony."

"Why did you pick that to tell her?"

"Because telling her the truth would take too long in a text," Bryce said.

Joe pulled a string hanging from a single bulb above his head. The yellow light barely had any effect on the dark.

"So what is the truth?"

He looked from me to Bryce and back again. Neither of us said anything.

"If you aren't going to tell me, I'll have to call your parents to take you back to school." He reached into his pocket for his phone and let his finger hover over the screen.

Bryce got up and pushed his hair away. "This is why."

Joe's eyes popped when he saw the bruise. He winced and touched his own cheek, then reached out to Bryce with his hand cupped. Bryce's forearm shot up to block him and he ducked. An awful sound came from his gut—part whimper, part grunt—and my heart shattered.

"I wasn't—" Joe said. "I'm sorry."

Bryce straightened slowly. "I know."

"Who did that to you?"

Bryce looked away, his expression stony.

"Who did it?" Joe asked again.

"You know who," Bryce said.

Joe's hands clenched and unclenched. "You never told me."

"I know."

"Did you tell anyone?"

Bryce kept his eyes cast down. The music changed to Spanish news, and dust drifted slowly from above.

"It isn't your fault," Joe said. "It isn't your shame to own."

Bryce pushed hay around with the tip of his boot, his

hands in his pockets and his yellow hair falling over his face again.

"You're not going to call him, are you?"

"As an adult, I'm supposed to report him. You need to get somewhere safe."

Bryce flung his head up. "Don't. Please. I'm leaving. I'm going back to Wyoming. My mom is coming to get me and Tuck, and if my dad finds out before she gets here, he'll find a way to stop her. You can call her. She's making the arrangements now. But please, don't tell my dad you know."

The lightbulb crackled, then sputtered, then went out. No one moved. Bryce watched Joe's face, his eyes pleading. Finally, after Joe had clenched and unclenched his fists a dozen more times, he nodded.

"I'll call your mom."

We followed him down from the loft and waited outside the office while Joe talked to Bryce's mom. We could hear his voice but not the exact words until the end when he said, "I'll make sure he's safe until you get here." When he finally came out of the office, his eyes were red.

"Okay," he said. "But you have to promise if he does it again before you can get out of here, you'll call me. Deal?"

"Deal."

We spent the rest of the afternoon helping Robert and Luis get the barn swept and putting feed in the horses' buckets before they were brought inside from the fields. We were almost done when Joe called us into his office.

"There are a couple of journalism students here from the high school. They're doing an article on community spirit and want to take pictures of some kids and horses. I figure you don't wanna do it, huh?"

Bryce shrugged. "Nah."

"Could I have mine taken with Fire?"

"Of course. You'll have to catch him, but bring him up and they'll get some shots."

The way Fire trotted to the gate when he saw me was exactly what I needed to get my mind cleared. I unwrapped a peppermint for him, then slipped the halter over his head and led him up the lane toward the barn. The two journalism students watched from the top of the hill.

"Love your pony," said the girl with the camera.

For those few minutes it took to lead Fire into the barn, take off his blanket, and comb out his mane and forelock for the picture, he wasn't just the pony of my heart. He was really mine.

Later, Mr. McDaid picked up Bryce and me at the regular time to go to the polo matches. We sat in the back seat silently while Mr. McDaid yakked on and on about a sailboat he wanted to buy for him and Bryce to use in the summer. Bryce stared straight ahead, poker-faced, and never said one word.

After the polo match, when Mom and I were both home, I told her what had really happened.

"I'm sorry I lied in the text," I said.

She tucked a piece of loose hair behind my ear. "You know how I feel about lying, but under these circumstances, I think you handled this very well."

"How?"

"You made sure I knew in case the school called, which they did. And you protected your friend by giving him privacy."

"What did you tell the school?"

"That it was an excused absence and I was sorry I didn't tell them in advance."

"You're learning how to tell white lies a lot better, Mom."

"I have an excellent teacher."

We were sitting side by side on the bed. In the soft light, Mom's skin had that peach-colored glow that always made her blue eyes look bigger. She was so pretty, it was hard to imagine Dad picking someone else. I leaned my head on her shoulder.

"Even after everything he did to us, at least Dad never hit us."

Mom stiffened, then kissed the top of my head. "The important things look a little different through someone else's eyes, don't they?"

"I guess."

"I had a call from my lawyer today. Dad's lawyer contacted them and asked if Dad could see you," she said softly.

"What did you say?"

"I told them it was up to you, and I would speak to you and let them know."

The heater cranked on and a puff of warm air made the yellow curtains in the window sway. My birthday gift, a reminder of something I loved from home. Seeing Dad was my choice now. Like that buck in the woods on Christmas day, I finally had power.

"Can I think about it before deciding?"

"You can think about it as long as you want. It's completely up to you."

TWENTY-EIGHT

The following Monday, I was watching lazy snowflakes drift from the sky outside the window when Ms. Fitzgerald tapped her knuckles on my desk. I had no idea what she'd been talking about because for three days I hadn't stopped thinking about Bryce.

"It is extraordinary," she said, "that one of our seventh graders wrote a poem good enough to not only qualify for the high school competition but to earn Honorable Mention. It is truly a gift."

Ms. Fitzgerald beamed at me. Every kid, in every chair, turned to stare. Jenna's mouth dropped open.

"I knew it!" she said. Her face was all lit up like she'd written the poem herself. "I knew you were a great poet!"

I slid further into my seat.

"Hello, earth to Lizzie!" Ms. Fitzgerald said. "I asked if you would read the poem to the class."

I begged her with my eyes not to make me do it, but her eyes begged me right back.

"I'm not comfortable reading my own poem out loud," I said. "Besides, everybody's probably already seen it."

Jenna nearly leaped out of her chair. "No, we haven't, Lizzie! And that's why we've been reading poems out loud to each other all year, just for moments like this. I say you read it. What about everyone else: Don't you think she should read it to us?"

There were scattered *yeah*s or *go for it*s from around the room. Danny rolled his eyes at Jenna and put his head down. "I'm takin' a nap."

Jenna didn't stop there. "Besides, we have to start reading our Partners in Poetry pieces next month. Since you're working by yourself, don't you want to practice?"

Danny raised his head. "Next month? I don't even know who my partner is!"

Ms. Fitzgerald looked around the room. "Seriously? Does everyone else know who their partner is?"

Jasmine raised her hand. "Danny's my partner."

"Oh, right. I forgot." He buried his face in his folded arms again.

Ms. Fitzgerald put her hand on my shoulder. "No worries, Lizzie, but do you mind if I read it to the class? It's really quite lovely."

I shrugged and sank lower.

Honorable Mention didn't come with money. That's all it meant to me now. I had only a little over a week before Mike made Joe sell Fire. Right that second, it was really terrible news.

Ms. Fitzgerald went to her desk, picked up my poem, and turned the page so everyone could see that the words were in the shape of an upside-down teardrop. Super. Just what I didn't need.

"This is a perfect example of a concrete poem style. See how it's shaped like a raindrop?"

Raindrop, not a teardrop. Good.

"Listen and you'll understand the creativity and thought Lizzie put into this style.

"Behind Birchwood

I dance around slippery rocks
blanketed in deep green moss,
jump last year's logs . . ."

She read the whole thing, start to finish, walking up and down the rows between the desks, performing like Jenna did when she read. Listening to someone else read the words I'd put on the page made it sound more like a real poet had written it. Like, maybe I was on the way to someday being as good as Robert Frost. Ms. Fitzgerald read the last line barely above a whisper.

"'Change is near.'"

She paused and looked around the room. All the kids were staring at me again.

"That's my favorite part," she said.

Jenna stood up from her desk and pumped her fist. "Oh, Lizzie! That. Is. Stellar!"

But all I could think about was how to make up that twenty-five dollars.

Joe said I could use the barn washers and dryers to earn more money, so I posted new signs around the barn and added *Laundering* to the list of services I offered horse owners. Over the next few days, more people signed up for tack cleaning. I wrote down the money in my notebook, but even though I hadn't quite reached my goal, there was something I just had to do.

I took the envelope with the one-hundred-dollar bill Mr. McDaid had given me and brought it to school. At lunch, I pushed it across the table to Bryce.

"What's that?" he asked.

"Open it."

He pulled out the Ben Franklin and held it up. "Huh?"

"Your dad put it in my jacket pocket on Christmas. I don't want his money. I figured it could help you and your mom."

"My dad gave you this?"

"Yeah. Now I'm giving it to you."

"What about saving for Fire?"

"Five more people signed up for tack cleaning. I'll save enough money the honest way. I want you to have that. This way your dad is helping pay for you to get home."

"Thanks, Lizzie. I know how much Fire means to you." He tucked the envelope into his jacket.

That evening, Bryce came to Fire's stall, where I was brushing out his tail.

"My mom is on her way," he said. "I'm leaving Sunday."

I'd known it was coming, but his words made my insides freeze.

"Sunday? Already?"

"Sunday. But I have an idea, a plan."

I didn't want a plan. I wanted him to stay. I wanted his dad to not be who he was so nothing had happened to make Bryce leave. I wanted to throw my arms around his neck and tell him how his friendship had kept me upright during the months since we'd known each other and I was so sorry he had to leave and I'd never forget him. Ever.

But I didn't do any of that.

Instead, I said, "A plan?"

He lowered his voice. "Can you sneak out from your house at night?"

"I did once. Why?"

"Can you meet me here tomorrow night, at midnight?"

"What's going on?"

"You trust me?"

"Of course," I said.

"Then come at midnight, right here by Tucker's and Fire's stalls, okay?"

"Can't you tell me why?"

"I can, but I won't. You'll see. It's a reverse going-away surprise. Okay?"

My stomach swooped up inside my belly. "Okay. Midnight. Tomorrow. Here."

He slipped out of the stall. I didn't see him again all evening.

At a quarter till midnight the next night, I bypassed the chestnut tree and went around to the old stone wall, traveling the path I could have walked blindfolded. From the woods, I could see a crack in the door to the barn. A single bulb cast a triangle of light across the snow-covered ring. I ran past it quickly, then flattened myself against the wall and peeked around the corner. No one in sight.

"Bryce?"

He came out of Fire's stall. "Come in. Hurry."

"What are we doing?"

He handed me a helmet and said, "Put this on."

"Huh?"

"You know the rule, no riding without a helmet. Put this on."

"Why?"

"We're going riding. We never got to ride together before, and now I'm leaving. So put the helmet on and let's get going."

"You're crazy," I said. "We can't do this."

"Why not?"

"Because—I don't know. Well, for one thing, I don't have my own horse to ride."

"Yeah, you do. Look behind you."

Fire already had his bridle buckled on. He was chewing the bit like none of this midnight stuff was a big deal.

"Get him and let's go," Bryce said. "Time's a wastin'."

"I'm going to ride Fire? Bryce, you're crazy!"

"Best kind of crazy you'll ever know," he said, grinning.

I didn't wait for him to say anything else. I lifted the reins over Fire's head and followed Bryce and Tucker to the outdoor ring. The snow came up well past Fire's fetlocks.

"We're going to leave tracks," I said.

"Last time anyone except you or me was out here was in the fall. No one will see them," he said.

"Are you sure about this?"

"One hundred percent."

"No one's ridden Fire except Joe. What if he's too much for me?"

"Not true. Joe let me ride him the other night. You'll be safe."

"You rode him?"

"I did. He was a perfect gentleman."

"Bryce—" I started, but there really wasn't anything to say. I patted Fire's neck then gathered the reins in my hand. "Of course he was a perfect gentleman. What was I thinking?"

I pushed myself off the ground, swung my right leg over his back, and settled into the saddle. I'd dreamed of this for so many months, but until that warm simmering feeling spread throughout my body, I hadn't known how perfect it would be. I laid my cheek against Fire's thick yellow mane and closed my eyes, knowing there would never be words perfect enough to describe how it felt.

"Ready?" Bryce asked.

I sat up and gathered the reins, not caring that he could see a tear streaming down my cheek.

"Totally ready," I said.

We rode past the stone wall, past the place where I had made my own trail to and from the chestnut tree, turning right into the thick of the woods. Fire and I trailed behind Tucker and Bryce for at least ten minutes until the density eased and the trees opened to a gentle, sloping hill and a large field of unbroken snow. Everything, from the sky to the ground, was white and navy. Fire's back swayed side to side as we made our way carefully down the hill. At the bottom, Bryce pulled Tucker up and motioned for me to come next to him. His face looked both pained and happy, crushed and excited at the same time.

"You understand why I have to leave, right?"

I nodded. "I'm glad you told your mom. It was the only way to get out."

Bryce ran his fingers through Tucker's mane, then looked at me, his eyes serious. "Remember what you just said. The part about speaking up. It took a lot of punches before I had the guts to call my mom. It's going to be hard to not feel like what he did was my fault, but it wasn't. It's his problem. My head already knows that, not so much the rest of me. But I'll get there. So will you, someday."

I looked up, startled.

"I—"

He waved his hand to stop me, and I let it go. There wasn't anything that needed to be said. Bryce knew me. He'd nailed it. Exactly. He'd given me a key.

"Hey, wanna canter up the hill?" he asked.

"You think it's safe? Fire won't take off bucking?"

Bryce tilted his head. "Lizzie, it's you riding him. You're his human. He won't ever do anything to hurt you."

"You're right," I said. "Let's do it."

"Ladies first."

Tucker didn't want ladies to go first. He pranced in circles like he was a polo pony before the start of a match, pulling against Bryce's hands holding the reins. I turned Fire toward the top of the hill.

"Now?"

"Now!"

I didn't even need to squeeze my legs; Fire's energy told me he was ready to go. The second he felt my grip on the reins soften, his front legs rose, he pushed off with his hind-quarters, and we glided into a perfect and powerful canter. I leaned forward, twisted my fingers into the feathery softness of his mane, and together, with snow flying up around us, Fire and I floated to the top of that hill like we were one. It was a dream come true, like a promise that nothing bad could ever happen again.

TWENTY-NINE

Bryce, his mom, and Tucker pulled out of the Birchwood driveway just after dawn on Sunday, heading over two thousand miles to Wyoming. Joe and Kennedy and I were all there to say goodbye. Mr. McDaid was not.

"We have to go a roundabout way to avoid some of the mountain passes in the snow, but we should be home by Thursday," his mom had said.

She looked exactly like Bryce, with yellow hair, green eyes, and high cheekbones. When she hugged me and thanked me for being there for Bryce, the fear I'd felt over losing my best friend was replaced with happiness for Bryce and for his mom. The loss to me was great, but the joy for Bryce was greater.

Bryce hugged me with one arm. "Stay out of trouble," he said, grinning. "And I'll buy you a front-row seat when I'm in the Olympics."

"I'm counting on it," I said softly.

After the trailer was out of sight, I went to Fire's stall for comfort. The one-hundred-dollar bill I'd given Bryce was tacked to the front with a note.

Keep it to buy Fire. We're okay. Now it comes from me.

Thanks. B.

On Monday, I sat alone at our table in the cafeteria, smelling ammonia and smashing mashed potatoes with the tines of a fork until they looked like a giant striped pancake. I was wondering how far Bryce might have gotten in the twenty-four hours since he'd been gone when Jenna dropped her tray onto the table and sat in his seat.

"Hey," she said. "You okay?"

Whenever Jenna asked a question, she scrunched her face up so her freckles bunched together.

"Yeah."

"I heard Bryce moved away."

"How did you hear that already?"

Jenna raised her shoulders and twisted her mouth. "His dad lives next door to us."

"Oh, I didn't know."

"Yeah, I saw you there on Christmas. I wanted to come say hi, but we weren't invited, so I didn't. My parents don't like Mr. McDaid very much."

"He's a complicated man," I said.

Jenna had three desserts on her tray and no real food. She started in on a piece of chocolate cake.

"Did you already eat your lunch?" I asked.

"What do you mean? This is lunch."

"It's all dessert."

She looked at her tray like this revelation surprised her, and grinned. "I'm not allowed to eat this kind of stuff at home. My mother is a health nut and my father doesn't pay attention to anything except his job, so I eat dessert here."

"Huh. I never noticed," I said.

"Probably because we never ate lunch together before, so how would you know?"

She scooped a spoonful of chocolate pudding from a dish and plopped it on top of berry pie, then cut a big forkful and offered it to me.

"No thanks."

"You sure? It's really good."

I looked around the cafeteria at all the kids I knew nothing about. What they ate, where they lived, who their friends were, what their parents were like. It had been almost six months that I'd been in this school with my head down.

I smiled at her. "I'm sure, but thanks anyway."

That afternoon when I got off the bus, I trudged the half mile to my road, still thinking about Jenna. I'd never really noticed before how lonely she looked. Did Bryce even know she lived next door to him? And if I hadn't noticed that Bryce had bruises and Jenna was lonely, what else was I not seeing?

I crossed to the other side of Brook Drive, cut the corner through the snow, and stayed flush against the brushy trees. It was a habit so no one passing by might see me going to Good Hope.

"Lizzie!"

I turned quickly, and there he was, standing on the opposite corner, waiting for me just like he used to when I first started kindergarten, on special days when he would take an early train home to surprise me. He looked exactly the same, from the way his dark hair was cut short to his freshly shaven face. Even from across the road, I imagined I could smell his menthol shaving cream. When I was little, he used to let me sit on the edge of the sink and swirl my grandfather's brush around in a cup, then dab minty foam all over his face before he scratched away black stubble with a razor.

"Lizzie," he said again, softer this time. "It's me."

My tongue was pinned to the roof of my mouth. When I was finally able to push words out, they didn't even sound like mine. "I was supposed to get to pick if I wanted to see you."

He started across the road until I put both hands up.

"Lizzie, I've waited so long," he said. "I couldn't wait anymore."

"Does Mom know you're here?"

I already knew the answer. Mom had given me the power to decide. She wouldn't take it away without talking to me first. Not Mom.

"I need to tell you something," he said. "I need to explain."

A silver sports car was parked about a half a block up the road. Through the window I could see the outline of the lady with blond hair poofing out around her head. She watched me watching her, then raised her hand and waved.

"Is that her?"

He glanced quickly over his shoulder, then came across the road anyway, his hands out, palms up, the way you get a frightened pony to trust you.

"Don't worry about her, Lizzie. She had the money to get me out of jail, that's all. I couldn't stand being in there. You have no idea what it's like to be confined."

My leg almost jerked out, aiming for his shin. "There are other kinds of confinement, Dad, so yeah, I know all about that."

"Sweetheart, I thought I'd get to see you if I was out."

"You were out. I waited. You never came. You got out before we even moved. You didn't even try to help us. You knew where to find me all along, but you didn't come."

"It's not that simple. Mom didn't want—" He glanced over his shoulder at the car and the blond lady waiting to save him again. "I'm sorry, Lizzie, so very sorry."

"Has the trial happened yet?"

He shook his head. "I've made a decision. That's why I had to come."

His eyes got wet, and he put two fingers to his chest, trying to press away something that hurt, the same way I always did. I knew everything about him—the shape of his nose, the way he tilted his head and closed his eyes when he pulled a bow across the strings of his violin, the specific way he bunched the couch pillow under his head when he was reading. I even knew that sometimes, on those Saturday mornings so long ago when it was his turn to make breakfast, he burned the bacon on purpose just to make me and Mom laugh.

"What, then?"

He shifted from one foot to the other. "I've decided to plead guilty."

My hand flew to my mouth. "Guilty?"

"I'm not going to fight it anymore. If I plead, I'll go to a prison that isn't as bad, and I'll be out in four years."

My legs trembled.

"I know that sounds like a long time, but if a jury finds me guilty, it could be fifteen. I can't do fifteen; you'll be all grown-up by then."

"Guilty?"

He nodded solemnly, his face grave, ashamed. He was afraid.

"Why didn't you tell me that from the start?"

"I didn't know what to say. It was all so wrong, but it was my wrong, not yours, not Mom's."

"It didn't feel that way."

His shoulders slumped, and suddenly he looked like an old man. "What's worse than facing prison is knowing how much I hurt you and Mom. I'll never recover from that."

"Guilty." I repeated his word again.

He was going to prison. Even after not seeing him for so long and wanting him to tell me the truth, the reality of his going to prison shocked me. And it hurt.

"Can I write you while I'm away," he asked. "Will you read my letters?"

"You can write," I said, trying hard not to let him hear my voice wobble. "Now I have to go."

He took another step toward me. I put my hands up and shook my head.

"Not now," I said. "I'm glad you told me but not now."

He made a noise when I turned away, but I kept going, shoulders back, head up, determined strides to at least look powerful, at least give the appearance of being in control. I kept it up all the way until I turned into the yard where he couldn't see me anymore. I dropped to my knees, covered my face with my hands, and let tears soak the mittens Mom had crocheted while sitting on the couch at Good Hope: A Home for Families in Transition.

THIRTY

The day before the deadline Mike had given Joe to put Fire up for sale, I walked to the thrift store and collected the rest of what was owed to me, then went back to Good Hope to count it all out.

"One thousand and one, one thousand and two, one thousand and three dollars!" I said out loud. "Oh my god, I did it. I did it!"

I had the money for Fire. He was actually going to be mine! I rubber-banded the bills into cylinders and stuffed them in my backpack, then ran through the woods so fast my feet barely touched the ground. By the time I got to the top of the hill and barged through the door to Joe's office, my lungs were on fire.

Joe leaped to his feet. "Lizzie, are you okay?"

I flopped into a chair and threw the backpack on his desk. "Oh, yeah, I am so okay. I'm great, Joe. Great!"

A lady standing off to the side stared at me with her mouth half open.

"Oh!" I sat up quickly. "Sorry. I didn't know you had anyone in here."

"Susannah," Joe said. "This is Lizzie."

"Oh, Lizzie," she said, like she already knew who I was. "Then I should wait outside."

She scooped a bunch of papers from the desk and put them into a folder. "Nice to meet you," she said. "I'll just be out here."

Joe nodded and held the door for her. As soon as it was closed, I dumped the rolls of cash onto his desk.

"Look! I've got it all! Every penny plus three extra dollars!"

Two cylinders rolled onto the floor. Joe picked them up and laid them with the rest of the money.

"What is all this, Lizzie?"

"For Fire! I got all the money before the end of the month like Mike said, so I can buy him!"

I pushed each bundle to make a pile in the middle of the desk and cupped my hands around them.

"What?"

"I did it, Joe, I made the deadline!"

I sat in the chair, my hands covering the money, and watched his face change from unbearably sad, to firm and resolved, then back to the saddest of sad. Suddenly, it felt like a bag of rocks had crashed over me.

"Lizzie—" he said. He glanced at the closed door. "Susannah—"

Everything froze inside me again. "Who is that lady?"

Joe moved his mouth like he was trying to make words come out, but they wouldn't.

"Tell me," I pressed him.

"Lizzie, I'm sorry. She is Fire's rightful owner. He isn't going to be sold to anyone. He has to go back to her."

"What?"

"Someone stole Fire from her and sold him at the sale. She wants him back. He has to go back."

"Back where?"

"Massachusetts."

"No, Joe. No."

"I am so, so sorry."

I stood up too quickly and my chair flew back against the wall.

"It's impossible," I said. "Look at all my money. We'll give it to her!"

I turned to the door to let Susannah back in, but Joe grabbed me and shook his head. His voice was soft and sad, the same way it had been the day he saw Bryce's bruise.

"We already tried. She's bringing her trailer on Saturday to take him home."

"No, this isn't true." Hot tears spilled down my cheeks and gathered into little puddles in the corners of my mouth. Joe's face swayed in front of me. "It's not fair!"

His eyes locked on mine. "It is true, Lizzie. It's horrible, but it's true."

"She can't just show up here and claim him and you just say okay. She has to have proof!"

"She has everything. Photos, his registration papers, and the police report. He belongs to her."

"But I spent all this time working to save money to buy him, and I never made anyone help me, and now he's supposed to be mine and you know it. You know it, Joe!"

I screamed that last sentence, then made a giant swath across the desk with my arm, spewing the rolls of money into the air. They hit the wall so hard, the rubber bands snapped. Green papers floated to the floor like feathers.

It had all been for nothing. I was losing him anyway. Joe tried to grab me, but I was too fast. I flung the door open, pushed Susannah aside, and was halfway to the woods by the time Joe got to the top of the hill. I raced past Fire's old paddock, past the chestnut tree, and through the woods with great sobs bursting from my chest. My feet pounded the earth, my legs pushed harder, faster, until they ached, but I couldn't stop until I got to Good Hope and barreled through the back door. When I got to our room, I threw myself face-first onto

Mom's bed, screaming into her pillow.

"No! No! No! No!"

It had all been for nothing. Every dream I'd had, every penny I had earned, every moment I'd spent daydreaming about how Fire would be mine—none of it mattered. Nothing mattered. Nothing at all. And no amount of crying was going to change the truth.

Kennedy came to Good Hope an hour later. By that time, I was up and pacing between the window and the bunks, my arms crossed tight in front of my chest, trying desperately to figure a way to keep Fire, and mourning that I hadn't even gone to see him before I left.

"I heard," Kennedy said when she came into the room. "I'm so sorry."

"How can it be true?"

"I wish I had an answer. I've had this happen so many times. I can't count how many horses I've loved that got sold out from under me. I know how you feel. I'm so sorry."

I threw my arms up in the air. "Did you work a million hours to save money for a horse?"

She shook her head. "No, I didn't have your courage. But I've loved at least a dozen the same way you love Fire. They were all taken from me, sold to someone else. It hurts just the same."

"My father did something really bad, Kennedy. That's why we ended up here. He stole money from his company. I didn't steal anything. I earned every penny of that money myself! And in the end, it didn't matter anyway. It's so unfair!"

Whether because I was mad or because I'd already told Bryce, it was easier this time telling Kennedy about what my dad had done. But what I'd said was true—in the end, it didn't matter. None of it mattered anymore.

Kennedy put her hand on my shoulder. "Everyone ends up here for one reason or another. I'm sorry about your father. You know my story, and if it weren't for Jamie, I'd assume all fathers were bad. But you can't let their stuff ruin you. You're better than that. You have to rise each time they push you down. You have to rise each time you fall."

I spent every minute I could over the next two days with Fire. Joe let me off work, and no one bothered me. Word spread quickly throughout the barn that I had tried to buy Fire, but he was leaving. On Saturday morning, I left Good Hope before sunup, when only a spoonful of gray light hovered over the hill. It was too early for Miss May to be there, so I didn't sign out. Mom knew where I'd be. Other than her, I didn't care. I stopped to pour a packet of instant oatmeal into the bird feeder, then stepped down the path and took a right at the fork for the last time.

Lime-green shoots and purple crocus buds were trying hard to poke through lingering crusts of snow framing the edge of the trail. I crouched beside them and wiped the white crystals off so the sun could help them open. When I got as far as the chestnut tree, I leaned my forehead against the trunk, closed my eyes, and wished some of that tree's stamina could peel off like bark and cover me with courage. Just for today. Then I moved quickly down the hill and up the lane to the barn. Fire and I had only a few hours left. Susannah was coming at nine.

At 8:35, I was sitting on the floor in the corner of Fire's stall, his head lowered in front of me so I could scratch behind his ears, when Kennedy came in.

"Susannah's here," she said. "Early."

"Couldn't she at least have waited until nine like she said?"

"I don't know, kiddo. Maybe she thought it best to get it over with."

"I'm not ready."

"You'll never be ready. Give yourself a minute. I'll distract them so they don't come looking for you."

I got up anyway and wrapped my arms around Fire's neck. "There's nothing that's ever happened in my life that's worse than giving you up," I said into his ear. "Nothing."

He pushed me with his muzzle when I clipped the lead rope to his halter and led him from the stall toward the other end of the barn. We walked slowly up the aisle, my eyes on the ground, my ears listening to the sounds of his hooves clomping on the concrete. One-two-three-four. One-two-three-four. The most beautiful music in the world.

Outside, the sun shined shamefully bright. Susannah

stood by the back of the trailer with Mom, Joe, Kennedy, and Jamie. Her eyes were as blue as Mom's, and the way she smiled at me, I knew that what was happening hurt her, too. It was completely different from what I was experiencing, but she understood. It was a comfort to know that if Fire had to leave Birchwood, at least he was going back to someone he already knew, to somewhere he'd already called home.

Mom rubbed the end of Fire's nose. "Thank you," she said. "Thank you for watching over my little girl."

Jamie put his hand on my shoulder. "I'm sorry, Lizzie."

I buried my face in Fire's mane again and cried for the pony who had needed me at the exact same moment I needed him. "Never, ever forget," I whispered.

Then I handed the lead rope over to Susannah and backed away to let her load him. He stepped into the trailer like he'd done it a hundred times before. When Susannah was tying his lead rope up front, Kennedy peered closely at Fire's tail, glanced at me, and grinned. Inside my jacket pocket, my fingers clasped a roll of silky custard-colored hair I'd cut out of his tail that morning. It was all I had left.

"Good work," Kennedy said quietly. "I've done the same thing myself."

Susannah latched the trailer door so all I could see of Fire were the very tops of his hindquarters.

"Is there anything I can do for you, Lizzie?" Susannah asked.

Yes! Leave him here. Don't take him away.

"Can you tell me his name? The one before Fire?" I asked.

"He's called Quixote, after one of my favorite characters in literature."

"Don Quixote?" Mom asked.

"Yes, the errant knight who made impossible dreams come true."

My heart warmed, and even though I didn't want to, I smiled. "He lived up to his name, then. Thank you."

Susannah jingled her keys in her hand. "Well, then, I should go."

I snuggled into Mom's arms and watched the trailer move slowly up the driveway, waiting for the anguish I knew was going to flood me any second. The right blinker came on, and just as Susannah turned onto the road, Fire whinnied. He whinnied so long, and so loud, the earth vibrated under my feet. I bolted away and ran down the lane toward the woods, my hand wrapped in the silkiness of his tail, smiling through my tears, because I knew, once again, that he was calling for me.

THIRTY-ONE

Kennedy came to see me again that night. We sat on Mom's bed and looked at a scrapbook with pictures and mementos from all the horses Kennedy had loved. She talked a lot about losing her mother and about the fire that gave her Jamie.

"My life is like the mythical phoenix bird that rose from literal ashes," she said. "Yours will be, too. You're on the verge of that part. Don't waste your time sitting in this room and feeling sorry for yourself. Come back to Birchwood soon. Your family is there."

Before she left, she laid my backpack on the bed.

"The money is all here," she said. "That's crazy-hard work you did, kiddo. If nothing else, be proud."

Mom stayed with me all day Sunday. I watched from my bunk as she rearranged the drawers three times—until finally everything was back the way it was before she started. At five o'clock she went to meet Mrs. Ivanov in the common room.

"Want me to come get you for dinner?"

"I'm not hungry," I said.

"You have to eat. I'll smuggle something in later."

She was back in an hour, tapping on the door with her foot. I crawled down from my bed and opened it wide, but it wasn't Mom. It was Leonard. He stood in the hallway holding a miniature peach rosebush and a yellow envelope.

"Oh! I thought you were my mom!"

His eyes searched my face for something, then he held out the plant.

"It's what I could do," he said.

"What?"

"About the horse and your friend who had to left. I am sad for you. I brought this from my job, the greenhouse. We planted all winter. I saved this one for you."

A miniature peach rosebush. He was sad for me. He was kind. No words would come.

"A little money I save to help you buy the horse," he said. "It's in the card. Keep it. You'll find different one someday."

Then he turned and walked away.

When Mom came back with a paper plate of dinner, I was sitting by the window, staring out into the dark, the peach rosebush in my lap. The light shined behind me, casting my reflection on the glass.

"Hi, sweetie. How are you?"

I touched a fingertip to a peach rose blossom. "Look what Leonard brought."

She leaned over and put her nose up to a bloom. "Mmmm, yummy. That was so thoughtful."

"I didn't know he worked in a greenhouse. I feel terrible. I always thought he hated me."

"Don't be too hard on yourself. Sometimes, when we don't understand something, we make judgments about people that aren't accurate. That's why it's always important to keep your eyes, ears, and mind open."

"He always talked like he was angry at me or thought I was stupid."

She massaged her fingers into my shoulders and smiled at me in the glass.

"Maybe you misjudged him because his accent is different. It can sound a little harsh, but that doesn't mean he's harsh. It's just not what you're used to."

"Maybe."

Mom came around and perched on the windowsill. "I think if you open your heart just a teensy bit and look around, you might see a lot of things differently."

A ladybug crawled out of the rosebush and onto my

fingernail. "We should make a wish."

"A wish, yes. Let's make a wish," Mom said.

We both closed our eyes. For so long, I'd put everything I had into saving money for Fire, and now it took me a second even to come up with something else I wanted. Finally, I wished for Mom to be happy again. But when I opened my eyes, I saw that my wish had already come true. Mom *was* happy. I'd just never noticed. She was at peace.

"I need to tell you something, Mom. Angela's been paying me to babysit. I know you thought I was just being nice, but I wasn't. She was paying me. I'm going to give her back all the money, then the rest of what I earned I'm giving to you to pay some bills."

She leaned over and smoothed my hair back from my face. "Give the whole thing to Angela if you want. We're going to be fine, and I'm afraid her back-on-her-feet is going to take a lot longer than ours."

She smiled and kissed the top of my head, then went to get dressed for bed.

That night I put all the money into a gallon-sized plastic baggie I confiscated from the kitchen and taped it to the counter in the bathroom with a note.

Dear Angela,

Here is the money you paid me plus some more I earned over the winter. I want you to have it all. My mom says we'll be leaving Good Hope when we are back on our feet, but we are worried your "back on your feet" is going to take longer, so I want you to have this money to make that happen sooner. Thank you for being my friend.

Lizzie

On Monday morning, I waited for the bus at the corner of Good Hope and Brook Drive, where I was supposed to be getting on and off all year. The driver almost drove right past, but I leaned into the road and flagged him down. The wheels and brakes squealed to a stop. I figured he would say something nasty about my doing that, so I kept my eyes down and took my place alone in the front-row seat.

"Hey," he said.

"Yes?"

"All year I've been waiting for the kid who was supposed to get on here. Why'd you walk all the way down to that other stop?"

I looked at him without saying a word. The tiniest smile curved on his lips for the very first time.

"Got it," he said. "But there's no shame in needing a little help sometimes."

He said that last part at the same time he pulled the squeaky door closed so no one else would hear.

After third period, I stopped at my locker to get my history book. Two plastic grocery bags were looped around the lock. A folded, handwritten note was taped on the front of one bag.

Lizzie,
We're really sorry about Bryce leaving and about Fire. Really, really sorry. Rikki saw you come to her dad's thrift store the day you sold your stuffed animals. We really liked them, so we each bought one. Yesterday we all decided that you should have them back, so here they are. Hope they help make you feel better.
Rikki Sabrina Jasmine Jade

My stuffed animals were in the plastic bags. The panda had a purple ribbon around his neck. Other than that, they were exactly the same. I ran all the way to class, hoping to sneak in before they got there and hide in the back corner while I figured out what to say. They'd beat me to it. Eight eyes were glued to the door when I walked in.

Jade nudged Rikki. "She's here."

All four girls quickly became very interested in their homework notebooks or something in the bottom of their backpacks, pretending they didn't see me cross the room. I stopped in front of their desks and fumbled with the zipper of my backpack. A tiny clump of stuffed golden retriever hair was stuck in the teeth. I kept fumbling until Jasmine spoke up.

"You okay?"

"Yeah," I said. "Yeah, I am okay. Thank you. I really mean it."

I scooted past and escaped to my solitary desk, wondering if they would have done something so nice if they'd known I was one of the homeless people they had cautioned me about.

By the end of the day I was so wrung out, if it hadn't been for English class and Ms. Fitzgerald, I would have gone to the nurse's station and pretended to have a headache. I slipped into my chair silently, got out my notebook, and drew a picture of a girl taking a nap instead.

"So today is the day!" Ms. Fitzgerald said brightly. "First week of March, the month of our Partners in Poetry Project. Are you all as excited as I am?"

Danny's head flew up, and he looked back at Jasmine. "Huh?"

"Don't worry, I gotcha covered."

He gave her a thumbs-up and laid his head down again.

"Does anyone want to volunteer to go first tomorrow? Or do I need to assign a team?"

Jenna's hand flew up. "We'll go!"

Her partner, Brenda, grabbed Jenna's hand and slammed it to the table.

"No. We. Will. NOT!"

"Why not?" Jenna whined. "We're totally ready!"

"I don't care. Only nerds go first."

"Oh, for goodness' sake, why are you so worried about something that stupid?"

"See? This is why I should have been partnered with Jasmine. She knows this stuff."

The whole class watched while Jenna and Brenda hashed it out. In the end, Jenna lost the battle.

"So stupid," she said.

"Okay, so not Jenna and Brenda. Anyone else? Any takers?"

After the episode that labeled whoever went first as a nerd, not one person raised a hand. Being called a nerd didn't bother me, but I was the only one who had written a poem without a partner and was going to stand in front of the class and read it by myself. I was not volunteering.

"Well, I anticipated this, as you might have guessed, so I have every student's name in this bowl. Danny? Will you come up front and pick names for the first people who will present tomorrow?"

"Huh? What am I supposed to do?"

"Come on," Ms. Fitzgerald said, jiggling the bowl. "Come up and draw a name."

Danny stumbled his way to Ms. Fitzgerald and dug his hand deep into the bowl of little pieces of paper. He pulled one out and handed it to her.

"Lizzie," she said, smiling. "It's you. You will present your original poem and visual aid tomorrow."

* * *

After everything else that had happened over the past few weeks, reading my poem out loud didn't send me into a tailspin like I thought it might. That's not to say I was prepared, because I still hadn't written the poem I knew I was meant to use. And I had no idea what sort of visual aid to provide. I'd been counting on seeing what other people did for theirs before deciding on my own. But, without spending my afternoons at Birchwood anymore, I had all the time in the world to decide once I got home to Good Hope.

The next day, instead of going to sit in the cafeteria, I took my poem and sketch to the main office and asked for Miz Bee.

"Hi, hon, how are you?" she asked, pushing a new pair of silver-framed cat-eye glasses up the bridge of her nose. The fourth finger on her left hand sported a new ring with a humongous purple amethyst surrounded by dozens of tiny chip diamonds.

"Fine, thank you," I said. "That's a beautiful ring. It matches the school colors."

Miz Bee blushed and held her left hand out, fingers extended, so she could admire it herself. "Yes, my honey finally proposed. He knows me so well. And who'd have thought I'd get a second chance at love after all these years? There's hope for us all, I suppose. Now, what can I do for you?"

I carefully slid my sketch pad out of my backpack and flipped to the page I needed copied.

"Can you enlarge it for me? It's for my English class."

Miz Bee's eyes scanned the paper left to right, and her mouth dropped open. "Oh, my, this is lovely. I can, but I have to tear the paper out of the book to do it, is that okay?"

"Yes," I said, ripping it along the edge.

"How big?" Miz Bee asked.

"I'm not sure, um, poster size? It has to clip onto a stand like the size you put one of those big pads of paper on when you're up at the front of the class so everyone can see."

"Like a flip chart?" she asked.

"Yes! Exactly like a flip chart."

I handed her the piece of paper. She held it carefully in her hands and walked away. "Let's see if I can do justice to this."

Miz Bee brought my poem back sealed inside a plastic cover with a piece of cardboard to keep it from getting wrinkled.

"It's not quite as big as a flip chart, but it's the best I could do without distorting the drawing," she said.

"Thank you."

"And, Elizabeth," she said, beaming. "Good luck. It's beautiful. We're mighty proud to have a real poet here at our little school."

As soon as I got to Ms. Fitzgerald's room for last period, she motioned for me to go to see her at her desk.

"I know you wanted to work on this project alone, Lizzie,"

she said. "But I want to be sure you feel comfortable today."

"I'm okay," I said. "But thank you. I'm glad to get it out of the way."

"I am sure your poem merits more confidence than that."

"It isn't the poem itself. It's just the, um, you know, like being . . ." I pointed to the spot where we stood to read someone else's poem but where today I would read my own, along with exposing much more about myself than I ever expected to. "I mean it feels, um—"

"Feels like you are making yourself vulnerable in front of your peers. Is that what you mean?"

"Yeah, pretty much."

"Yup, I get it. That's why we usually do it in pairs. But you know what, Lizzie? You've been flying solo for a long time now. You already know how to soar."

I went to my seat while the other kids filed in and tried to sort out exactly how soaring tied in with reading my poem. Jenna sat down and leaned into the aisle between our desks to give me a thumbs-up.

"You'll do great today, Lizzie, I know it!"

Ms. Fitzgerald blew three notes on her wooden flute, signaling to the class that everyone should be quiet.

"So, fine and budding poets, today is the day. I want you to know that months ago, when we first discussed our original poetry projects, Lizzie came to me and offered to do hers on her own since we have an odd number of students—both the poem part and the visual aid. As the rest of you will discover as the weeks go on, standing up here and reading your original work with a partner beside you still feels like walking barefoot through a fire. Lizzie will be sharing her work by herself, so please give her the respect she deserves. Lizzie? You ready?"

I carried the plastic-covered poster up front and slipped it out with my back to the class. Everyone got quiet while I clipped it to the easel. Even Danny was sitting up watching me. Ms. Fitzgerald smiled and nodded for me to go. I took a deep breath, turned the easel so the class could see, and began to read.

I
step
into the forest and
press my foot upon the soft
earth of a path that winds through
the woods. At the split in the trail I stop to
catch my breath, fingering waxy honeysuckle vines,
remembering another route I used to walk that began
and ended with this same sweet aroma. Someone else leaves
footprints on that other path now. Someone else lives in our old
house, sleeps in my room, gazes out my window at the red maple tree
where my grandparents' ashes lie waiting for me to return.

But I know we will never be going home.

I found comfort and shelter under this canopy of cedar, birch,
and oak. I made peace with my life in transition under the powerful
gaze of a buck in winter who championed the change he saw in me.
In secret, I fed those in need: chickadees; a hungry dog; a frightened
pony, displaced like me; a friend starving only for someone to see,
who fed me, too, because that's what friends do. Now I wear new
shoes that let me fly down this path, once edged with maidenhair ferns,
then blanketed with musty fallen leaves, a landing place for snow,
pristine and white, like an invitation to make tracks, to reconnect,
and to discover finally it was me all along who was in need
and that I am ready now, to not fly solo anymore.

THIRTY-TWO

The next day when I got home from school, the baggie with all the rolls of money was taped to the bathroom counter, along with a folded piece of paper.

Dear Lizzie,

Your sweet note made me cry, in a good way. I'm so sorry about your friend, and the pony, and everything else. But I can't take this money. If I wasn't paying you, I would have to pay someone else and my girls might not like a different person. There are things in life much more precious than money, and for me, it's my girls. I want you to keep this for yourself. For a rainy day.

Love, Angela

That night I tucked the golden retriever under my arm and went to the common room looking for Mom and Mrs. Ivanov. Mom was sitting alone in front of the big window, weaving lilac-colored yarn around her finger and pushing the hook through to bring up loops. I plopped down next to her.

"Hey, sweetie, want to learn?"

She held up what looked like might someday turn into a hat.

"Maybe."

I fingered a roll of dark apricot yarn in the basket. It was fuzzy and soft and reminded me of Fire's coat, so I stuffed it under a roll of chocolate brown.

"Where is Mrs. Ivanov?"

"Oh, I guess you've been a little out of the loop this week. She and Leonard moved to their own apartment."

"What? When?"

"They left Sunday night. Isn't that nice?"

"I didn't know they were leaving. I never thanked him for the rosebush."

"I'm sorry, maybe I should have said something. I thought that's why he brought it for you. A goodbye gift of sorts."

"I guess."

"Brad and his boys are moving into their own place next

week, too. Isn't that nice?"

I picked up the ball of chocolate brown yarn and shrugged. "Yeah, that's really nice."

"I had a call from your English teacher this afternoon."

"Ms. Fitzgerald? Why?"

She looped another piece of lilac around her finger and smiled. "She wanted me to know how proud she was of you reading your own poem by yourself and how moved she was by what you said afterward. She told me you were teary when you got the standing ovation."

I snuggled up against her shoulder. "Yeah. It was hard saying all that stuff in front of them."

"Can you share with me what it was?"

"I had to tell them what inspired the poem. I told them it was because some people only get to dream of having a home of their own. Sometimes people have to find a place that's special to them, like the woods are for me, and that's home for a while."

"Do you think they understood what you meant?"

"Ms. Fitzgerald understood. I like to think some of the others did, too. I don't want to hide it anymore."

"Did it give you peace to put it all out there like that?"

"I guess."

I leaned my head on her shoulder and hugged the stuffed dog tight. Mom wove another strand of lilac around and around, dipped the hook in and out, made loops and ridges and poetry with her hands.

"I also had a call from Joe today."

"I'm not ready to go back."

"Well, he needs some help with something special on Saturday and was hoping you'd come regardless of how miserable you are feeling."

"What kind of help?"

She handed me her phone. "Why don't you call him and find out?"

I looked at the numbers on the screen for a second, then punched in Joe's number. He answered on the first ring.

"Hi, Joe. It's me."

"Hey, kiddo, how are you?"

"I'm okay," I said. "Sort of."

"We miss you."

"Sorry."

"Anyway, you know that little redheaded girl, Georgia?"

"Yeah."

"Her parents are buying wicked old Bluebell for her."

"What? Why Bluebell? She's a reincarnated ax murderer."

"Go figure, right? But that kid loves that pony, so there you have it. Bluebell gets her own human."

"Jeez," I said. "There are so many ponies in the world to pick from. But I'm glad for her. And for Bluebell. Maybe she'll stop being so nasty."

"That remains to be seen," he said. "Anyway, I had to find a replacement school pony. I'm going to pick it up on Saturday. Kennedy is on her photography trip for finals, and I was hoping you could come hold down the fort for an hour or so in the morning until I get back. It'll be early, before the students come, but I need someone reliable in case I'm a little late. You don't have to work, just be here, oversee the new working students."

"Be there like the token grown-up? That's kind of funny."

"Makes perfect sense to me. Besides, you get to be in on a huge secret if you do it."

"What's the secret?"

"You have to agree first. It's big. Really big."

"Okay."

"Atta girl."

"So?"

"Jamie bought Kennedy a horse for an early graduation gift. I'm picking her up, too."

A jolt of happiness launched me off the couch. The basket of yarn tumbled to the floor.

"What? You're not kidding, right? You wouldn't kid about that. Oh, man, she's going to be so excited!"

"Yeah, she is."

"What is it? What breed? It's a mare? You said she. What color? She loves bays, you know. With white markings. Lots of chrome. Do you even know what kind of horse she wants? It has to be tall, at least sixteen hands—is it tall?"

Joe laughed into the phone. "Relax, relax. Trust me, I know exactly what kind of horse she wants. She's talked about it for years. We searched far and wide for this mare, and she is everything Kennedy ever dreamed of. You'll see Saturday."

"Oh, man, I'm so excited for her."

And I meant it.

In the week since I'd walked the path to Birchwood, the woods had come alive. Specks of emerald-green laced the tree limbs. Clumps of wild daffodils grew in sunny pockets along the trail, bright yellow with orange trumpets that smelled like clean linens. When I came up behind the double chestnut, a robin was tug-of-warring with an earthworm lodged into the mud by Fire's old paddock.

I walked slowly past the fields to the barn and pressed my hand to my belly to quiet the butterflies.

The two new working students were checking the lesson list in Joe's office when I went in.

"Hi," one said. "I'm Amelia. This is Erika."

"Hi, I'm Lizzie."

"We know. Joe said you would be here and could answer questions if we needed help. Is that all right?"

"Sure," I said. "What's up?"

"Winter tried to bite when we tightened her girth. We just wanted you to check and be sure it was done right."

"Did you ask Robert or Luis?"

The girls looked quickly at each other and blushed. "No, we didn't want them to laugh at us, so we decided to wait for you."

"Okay," I said. "Give me one second. I'll be right there."

I closed the door and looked around Joe's office. Neither

Joe nor Kennedy had ever laughed, or made me feel stupid, when I was new. They'd never made me feel I was anything other than one of them. I opened the working student logbook and signed in: *Lizzie St. Clair, 8:30 am.*

Winter's girth was so loose the saddle had already slipped to one side. "Don't feel bad," I told the girls. "She's an expert at blowing up her belly."

Back at the office, a lanky man waited in the doorway with a tiny girl clinging to his thigh. Blue eyes peeked out from under a scuffed green plastic helmet that had been tied under her chin instead of clipped with safety snaps. She toed the floor with worn-out paddock boots that were way too big.

"Hi, I'm Daniel and this is Emily English. She has her first lesson today. We're about an hour early, but she couldn't wait."

"I understand that completely," I said. "Joe's teaching the beginner lesson today. He'll be back soon."

"Is he a good teacher?" Daniel asked.

"The best," I said. "The very, very best."

I leaned close to Emily.

"I'm Lizzie."

Emily pushed her dad in front of her. He tried to pry her arms from around his leg.

"Come on, Em, you've been waiting so long for this."

I held out a peppermint. "It says on the list you get to ride Rusty today. I happen to know Rusty is particularly fond of peppermints. Wanna know how I know that?"

She edged a little closer.

"Because he was the first pony I ever rode."

Emily looked up at her dad and made her mouth into a tiny O.

"Where is Rusty?" she asked.

"Come on, I'll introduce you, and if you feel like it, you can give him the peppermint."

Rusty lived in Tucker's old stall now. I didn't want to know who was in Fire's, but my feet turned that way on their own. Fresh shavings bedded the ground, hay filled the rack, and a new purple bucket hung from the wall. Other than that, it was empty. Purple was Kennedy's favorite color. If her horse was moving into Fire's stall, it would be okay.

"Can I give him a candy?" Emily asked.

I took her hand and unfolded her fingers. "You have to hold your thumb in, like this," I said, showing her how to keep it flush against her hand. "That way he won't think it's a carrot. Then, we put the peppermint flat on your palm, and hold it up underneath his mouth, like this."

She tried to shrink back, but as I knew he would, Rusty gently lifted the peppermint with his lips and Emily giggled.

"It tickles!" she said, wiping her hand on her jacket.

"Thank you," Daniel said. "She needed someone like you today. I don't know the front end from the back end of a horse, so I was useless."

"Not useless," I said. "You're here."

Joe got back a few minutes later. He pulled the trailer

slowly down the driveway until the ramp was lined up with the barn door.

"Thanks for coming," he said when he saw me. "I ended up getting two extra!"

"There're four in there?"

"Yup. Wait, you'll see."

Amelia and Erika came out of the barn with lead ropes. "Can we help?"

"Sure," Joe said. "I'll give you the first two. They go up to the isolation barn. Any two stalls are fine."

First one out was a cute bay pony with a white blaze running down his face and wide black hooves.

"Little gelding to replace Bluebell," Joe said. "Hopefully he'll be more polite."

The next one was an old gray with knobby knees and a swayback but kind eyes and blue spots on the pink skin around his mouth. Erika took him, and she and Amelia walked side by side up the driveway toward the four-stall annex barn.

"Wait till you see this," Joe said.

He hooked open the inside metal doors that separated the front of the trailer from the back. Hooves pounded against the rubber mats.

"Easy, pretty lady," Joe said, his voice familiar, gentle, experienced. "Let's walk out front first. There ya go, good girl."

A tall, bright bay mare with long legs and a beautifully arched neck came down the ramp, prancing like she expected a crowd to clap for her. Her legs looked like they'd been dipped in white paint halfway to her knees. A white blaze started under her black forelock and traveled down to a point at the end of her chiseled nose. Large dark eyes darted every which way. Her nostrils flared, then she thrust her head into a small patch of grass.

"She's exactly what Kennedy has always talked about. She's beautiful!" I said.

"One hundred percent Thoroughbred, but you can clearly see the Arabian horse influence from her ancestry in her face and neck," Joe said.

"What's her name?"

"Registered name is Eclipse, but Kennedy can call her whatever she wants."

I patted the mare's sleek neck. "Eclipse. It fits. How old is she?"

"Only four. Never raced. Clean bill of health and a big project for Kennedy, but she's up to it. Think she'll approve?"

"Um, yeah, pretty much."

The last horse still in the trailer screamed and kicked the walls, shaking the whole thing from side to side. *Bam! Bam!*

"Who is that?"

Joe rolled his eyes and handed Eclipse's lead rope to Luis with instructions to put her in Fire's old stall. The horse in the trailer screamed again, sending shivers throughout my whole body.

"I think this last one has to go back," Joe said. "The seller must have given her a sedative to keep her calm while I tried her out, but it wore off about halfway home. I had to stop twice to get her lead rope retied in there. She's a beauty but way too wild for a school horse. I'll get her."

He disappeared into the back of the trailer.

"Easy, girl, easy now," he said. "Everything's going to be okay, easy."

BAM! A hoof hit the metal side of the trailer.

"Whoa. Easy, little lady, easy," Joe said. "That's a good girl, that's a good girl. You're home for now: nice oats, nice hay, you're okay—"

Hooves struck again, followed by a loud thud and a grunt coming from Joe. The trailer rocked, and a black mare bolted down the ramp. Her lead rope hung loose around her legs as she skidded to a halt on the asphalt. Her black eyes locked with mine, then she snorted and was off, galloping down the lane toward the woods, her silky mane and tail streaming out behind her. With every stride, she flung her head left to right and screamed like a wild stallion.

About halfway down, she hurtled through a gate into a field and raced from one end to the other, mud flying. She was magnificent, and she was terrified. I sprinted down the hill just as the mare charged out, turning toward the woods, her tail flipped up like a flag. Before she reached the end of the lane, she swerved right into Fire's paddock and slammed to a halt.

"Lizzie! Stop!"

Joe was yelling at me from the top of the hill, but I couldn't stop. No way. I'd seen the look in the mare's eyes. She was every bit as afraid as Fire had been when he first came. Every bit as frightened as I was the day Mom and I arrived at Good Hope. By the time I got to the paddock and shut the gate, she was standing in the corner, her side pressed against the fence, her body heaving. Red veins pulsed inside wide nostrils, and a long black forelock fell over the pencil-thin blaze of white on her face. She blew a loud snort, put her nose to the ground, and trotted with long graceful strides to the other side, then stopped, raised her head, and watched me.

Mud coated her legs up to her knees. Flecks of brown were splattered all through her tail. I put my hand out, palm up, offering her a peppermint. It was all I had. She examined me warily, then tightened her muscles and bolted past, kicking a back hoof so close that the air brushed against my cheek.

"Lizzie, get out of there!"

Joe limped down the lane, holding his leg where she had kicked him. Robert and Luis were right behind him. The mare stopped again, sweat shining on her onyx coat. She watched me from the corner, flicking her ears back and front, back and front. I waited, just like I'd waited for Fire. Finally, her shoulders relaxed and she lowered her head.

"Everything is okay, pretty girl," I said quietly. I took one cautious step toward her. "You're home now. You're safe."

The lead rope dangled from her halter.

"I know just how you feel."

I took another baby step.

One more and I stopped, giving her a chance to get used to my being so close.

"You're okay, pretty girl. Everything is okay," I cooed.

"Lizzie!"

The mare startled, flung her head, and tossed her forelock aside. A thin line of blood trickled down her face.

One more step. "I can get that cleaned up for you."

She eyed the peppermint in my hand. I forced myself to breathe slower, easier, even though my heart was pounding. Finally, she got the scent of the mint and reached her head toward me, sniffed, then lifted the candy with her lips and crunched.

The entire world stopped moving in that moment. My hand moved slowly, so slowly, under her chin, until I wrapped my fingers around the lead rope. Before she could pull away, I scratched her cheek, then behind her ears and in that place under her forelock where a pocket of hair was soft and curly.

"Easy, sweet girl. You were just afraid. Nothing wrong except you need a friend. I'm right here, right in front of you. I am your friend."

She lowered her head and wiggled her lips the same way Fire used to.

"I understand. This is your new home. You're safe here, sweet girl. I promise."

SUMMER

THIRTY-THREE

"Air-conditioning!"

I spread my arms wide and fell backward onto my bed in our new apartment, giggling out loud. Jamie walked by in the hallway carrying a giant box toward Mom's room.

"If I'd known you didn't have air-conditioning over there, I would have bought you a little window unit."

"Oh, no." I sat up and wagged my finger. "Miss May doesn't allow window units except in the common room. It jacks up the electric bill too much."

"Ah. Of course. You like your room?"

I looked around at the stark white walls, the plain beige

carpet, and the single window looking out to a courtyard of flower beds. "Best room ever."

After everything from storage was carried in from the moving truck, Kennedy brought us dinner from the pub. Joe came with a plant for Mom. Linda was working, but she had sent over toilet paper and chocolates. We all sat on our old kitchen chairs, using unopened boxes as tables.

"Mmmm, chicken tenders and honey mustard," I said.

Kennedy laughed. "You're going to turn into a chicken tender one of these days. It's all you eat."

"Not true," I said. "I only eat them from the pub. Nothing else compares."

"So," Kennedy said coyly, "guess what Ellie did to me today."

"Hmmm?"

She stood up and pulled her riding breeches down on one side, exposing the top of her hip. "She bucked me off, little brat!"

A large area had already turned purple and black. Mom's hand flew to her mouth. Joe rolled his eyes. Jamie glanced at Kennedy and kept eating.

"Doesn't that worry you?" Mom asked him.

Jamie shrugged. "She's been through worse; she'll survive."

Kennedy nudged me. "Can you feel the love?"

"Well," Jamie said, "if you're going to ride young horses that behave like rodeo broncs, maybe you should get one of those protective vests that three-day eventers wear."

"Not a chance," Kennedy said. "Besides, a vest only protects your ribs and back, not your hips."

Mom cut a dainty bite of chicken parmesan. "Speaking of rodeo broncs," she said.

Jamie cut a bite of his steak and dipped it into A.1. sauce. He was addicted to A.1. Kennedy claimed he even put it on his scrambled eggs.

"Um, hello?" Mom prodded. "Rodeo broncs?"

"Oh, yes, I nearly forgot." Jamie wiped his mouth with the corner of a napkin and laid his fork and knife neatly on his plate.

"Forgot what?"

"Wait for it," Kennedy said, grinning. "Wait for it. Tell her, Dad."

"Well. Did you like my new SUV?"

Kennedy rolled her eyes.

"Your SUV?" I asked. "Yeah, I guess. I mean sure, it's nice."

"The reason I bought it— I mean, there were a lot of reasons. One, so Kennedy could have my old car. I didn't like her driving around in that tiny death trap—"

"Dad!" Kennedy said sharply. "Stop with the death trap and get to it, would you?"

"Well, I got this specific SUV because I wanted something roomy enough for long trips. You know: leg room, luggage, all of that."

"Okay," I said.

"So you and your mother will be comfortable on our trip."

"Trip?"

"Dad! Spit it out so we can call Bryce, would you?"

"Bryce?"

Kennedy threw her arms up. "Yes! We're going to see Bryce!"

I jumped up and looked at Mom, then at Jamie, over to Joe, then at Mom again. All of them were smiling and nodding, and Mom had tears in her eyes.

"Wait, how did this happen? Kennedy, we're going to see Bryce!" I spun around and reached out to hug her.

"Careful," she said. "You're going to tip over the fancy furniture."

"Does he already know?"

"Of course he knows," Mom said.

"We all knew," Joe said, smiling.

"When are we going?"

"Next month," Mom said. "Last week of July, during the big rodeo."

"We leave the twentieth, drive three days, spend a week, then come back," Jamie said.

"Are you kidding me?"

"Not kidding," Kennedy said.

"I can't believe it! Are you coming with us?"

"Not on the driving part, thank the good lord," Kennedy said. "But I'm flying out for a few days while you guys are there. You and Bryce aren't going to ride in those mountains without me, you know, not a chance."

"Let's FaceTime him right now, can we?" I flung around to Mom and bumped the box I was using as a table. French fries scattered all over the floor. "Do we have internet here?"

"Do you really think I would move us out of Good Hope and not have the internet already set up for you?"

I touched my face and pinched my cheek.

"Internet, air-conditioning, my own room, and going to see Bryce, all in one day. It's more than I can take."

"The trip is a gift from Jamie," Mom said. "He wanted to do it for you."

"Thank you, Jamie, thank you so much. This feels like a dream."

"You've both survived a tough year, Lizzie. You've earned it," he said.

I touched my cheek again and looked around the room, at the boxes and bins and the giant mess from the move, and french fries scattered on beige carpet, and at the four most important people in my life: Mom, Kennedy, Jamie, and Joe. My eyes stopped when I got to Jamie, the thin, quiet man who had seen a tiny girl named Kennedy in the hospital after a fire and made her his own, and whose gentle way made Mom happy again. And Kennedy, who was trying to get Bryce on FaceTime for me, and had become the closest thing I'd ever had to a sister. And Joe, who had seen me longing to belong and made it happen. I thought of the troubled, winding path that had brought us here, to this new home, and friends, and a totally different life from what Mom or I ever could have imagined, and nothing in the world that had happened over the past year and a half mattered as much as all those things did. Nothing.

"Thank you," I said quietly to no one in particular. "For everything."

"Mom?"

Even with fresh white paint everywhere, my new bedroom was dark. Mom's room was right across from mine, but she couldn't hear me. I switched on the lamp, threw my covers back, and tiptoed across the hall. Her old bed was so big, it left only a narrow path between the sides and walls of the bedroom. Mom looked shrunken under the covers.

"Mom?"

"Hmmmm?"

"I'm not used to sleeping alone anymore."

"Mmmmm," she mumbled.

Then silence.

"I'm not scared. I'm just not used to it."

Silence.

Very gently, I laid the corner of the comforter back and slipped into the bed, then pulled the covers up to my chin.

"Mom?"

Silence.

"I just wanted to say thanks for being so strong. And I love you."

A week later I knocked on the front door at Good Hope, not sure if I was allowed to just walk in like before. Miss May peered out, then flung the door wide.

"Come in, come in," she said brusquely.

"Thank you." I wiped my paddock boots on the mat and stepped into the front hall. "My mom said you called and we have some mail?"

"Yes, come with me," she said. "You need to tell your mother she should have had it forwarded already."

I followed her along the hall to the kitchen. "Yes, she knows and says she is sorry for any inconvenience."

Mom hadn't really said that. I made it up. But it was easier that way.

"Are Angela's girls here?"

"No."

"Oh, okay."

"Wait here," she said. "I'll go get it from my office."

Miss May left the back way. A tiny girl with curly light-brown hair peered around the corner from the hall, clutching a plastic horse to her chest.

"Hi," I said.

Her eyes widened, but she didn't answer. I squatted to eye level and smiled.

"I like your horse. I had some like that, too."

She clutched it tighter, like she was afraid I might take it from her.

"I used to live here," I said.

She blinked.

"My name is Lizzie. What's yours?"

She pointed to my boots. "Horse," she said, barely above a whisper.

"Your name is Horse?"

She shook her head. "You have a horse."

"Oh, I see. I work at a stable and I ride, but I don't have my own horse. Not yet."

She thrust her index finger into her chest and said, "Ride."

"You want to ride a horse?"

The little girl barely tilted her chin, but it was enough for me to understand exactly what she meant.

Miss May startled both of us when she came back. The little girl took off down the hall.

"Here you go," she said, handing over a bundle of mail. "And I found this left behind. It was under the mattress of your bunk."

The horse book. The one from Dad that the thrift store couldn't sell. I held it in my hand for a second, feeling the weight of it and all that had come after, but then I handed it back to Miss May.

"I'd like to donate it," I said. "To that little girl who was just here, the one holding the plastic horse."

"Grace," Miss May said. Her eyes flickered with something soft. One side of her mouth twitched, and she looked wistful. "She's so tiny. It's always the little ones I worry about the most."

We stood like we had so many times before, in another awkward silence with me looking out the window at the cedar tree, trying to understand how I'd never noticed that Miss May worried about us. A finch darted in behind the tree, then flew away. Maybe the birds kept coming back, hoping I'd return to feed them.

"I'll give it to her," Miss May said, laying it on the counter.

"Thank you." I turned to go.

"Elizabeth," she said. "I do hope everything goes well for you and your mother. And don't worry. I won't forget to feed the birds."

She moved away and went to the counter to make coffee.

THIRTY-FOUR

Dear Dad,

Thank you for the letter. I'm glad everything is going okay. It's good to know the other people were nice when you first got there. I know from living at Good Hope that people can surprise you in a lot of ways if you let them.

Mom and I moved into a new apartment in June. We love it. There is even a flower garden, and I can walk to the barn. I guess you know Mom and Jamie are getting married on Christmas Eve, so we'll move again then, to his house, and I'll have a stepsister, Kennedy.

She's a photographer and horse trainer.

Mom, Jamie, and I drove to Wyoming to see my friend Bryce in July. He was my first friend here, and it was a great trip, even though it took so long to get there. We had to stop a lot for Mom to take pictures.

I started a program at Birchwood for kids who live at Good Hope. I had some money saved, so I used part of it to buy riding boots at a thrift store and a couple of new helmets. Joe, the stable manager, agreed to let me bring the kids over once a week for a riding lesson on a semiretired pony named Rusty. I think it's really made a difference to the kids, and I was happy to find a meaningful way to use the money.

There is a horse at Birchwood I named Promise. She's a beautiful black mare. She was really scared when she first came, and I was the only one able to connect with her and get her calmed down. Joe has been working with her since then, and I finally started riding her a few weeks ago. Joe promised he wouldn't sell her until I could buy her myself. I love her so much, and she loves me.

Mom and I drove to the old house. The people who live there now let us dig up some dirt from under the red maple. I think the part we got has Grandma's and Granddad's ashes in it, and I feel much better knowing they are back with us again. I keep the dirt in a wooden box that Jamie made as a gift when he asked me if he could marry Mom. I'd never heard of anyone asking a kid if he could marry her mom, but apparently there are a lot of things I never knew.

School starts on Monday. I'll be in eighth grade, but I get to take a high school creative writing class for poetry. I'm sending you a poem I wrote last year for an English project, and I'll have Kennedy take a picture of me with my horse when she is finally mine. Promise.

Love,
Lizzie

Author's Note

The number of school-age children in America who experience homelessness each year is staggering. It is a tragedy, and there aren't enough places to give them all shelter like Good Hope: A Home for Families in Transition. Although Lizzie didn't realize it until she had come to terms with some of the reasons she was there, kids like her are the lucky ones. There are many, many more who sleep in cars, under bridges, in stairwells, all while trying to succeed in school and maintain friendships without divulging their secret.

My children and I easily could have been Lizzie and Mom. When my sons were little, there were two times when we suddenly found ourselves without a home. This can happen in the blink of an eye, to people with good jobs and even coming from large extended families. Like us. Those factors did nothing to ease the shock and the shame I felt as I tried to figure out how to protect my children. I was a single mother, already working two jobs, and I was terrified. Both times this happened, minutes before we ended up sleeping in our car, someone reached out a hand and offered us temporary housing until we could get back on our feet. One place was a small single room above a store that was previously occupied by a large black snake, which—after he was removed—we gratefully accepted. The other was an empty room in a friend's home an hour and a half away from my children's school and my job. The three of us piled into sleeping bags on the floor and ate way too much take-out pizza. Because these people reached out to help us, we never went without a roof over our heads. Not so for far too many families in like circumstances.

Most recently, as an adult closing in on retirement age, I once again found myself in a precarious position without housing when the historic meadow cabin I loved and had rented for many years was suddenly sold just as winter was approaching. My sons are grown, so this time I had only myself to worry about, but it was still frightening and a shock. My very dear friend Bettina Whyte quickly offered me shelter and comfort in her lovely home for the winter, to get through an upcoming brain surgery and to finish writing this book. I had written part of *Georgia Rules* there under different circumstances, so I already knew it to be a place that fed and sustained my creative muse. Bettina opened her home to me for no other reason except that, underneath her businesslike exterior, lives one of the softest, most tender and gentle souls I have ever had the honor of knowing. It is the rare Bettinas of the world who offer shelter to the weary. I am eternally grateful to her for the roof over my head, the love that came with her gift, and the stunning mountain views that gave me strength, courage, and inspiration to help me plow through the many revisions of this book.

I have been one of the lucky ones.

Moving books by

NANCI TURNER STEVESON

HARPER

An Imprint of HarperCollins*Publishers*

www.harpercollinschildrens.com